NIGHT AND DAY

DELANEY DIAMOND

Garden Avenue Press

Night and Day by Delaney Diamond

Copyright © 2021, Delaney Diamond

Garden Avenue Press

Atlanta, Georgia

ISBN: 978-1-946302-44-1 (Ebook edition)

ISBN: 978-1-946302-45-8 (Paperback edition)

www.delaneydiamond.com

For all the women who are told that they're "too much," you deserve someone who's afraid to lose you, just as you are. Not as they want you to be.

Bang. Bang. Bang.

Rubbing sleep from his eyes, Anton rolled onto his back and squinted against the sunlight coming in through the curtains.

Bang. Bang. Bang.

The noise was coming from the front door. Someone was knocking. *Loud.*

Rolling onto his side with a groan, he checked the clock beside the bed. Seven-thirty on a Saturday morning. *What the hell?* Who would—

Bang. Bang. Bang.

Irritated, he tossed off the sheets and marched to the door with angry strides. The person on the other side better be dying, or they'd be getting their ass kicked.

Though pissed, he took the precaution of peering out the peephole to see who was attacking his door and was taken aback when he saw the petite woman out front. Wearing a baseball cap low on her head, he could tell she was attractive even through the distorted lens and the angry pucker of her lips.

"Open the door, Calvin!" she screamed. "I know you're in

there, and I'm not going anywhere, so you might as well come out." She started banging with her fist again.

How could someone so small make that much noise?

Anton swung open the door and her hand remained suspended in the air, mid-bang. Her eyebrows winged together in a startled expression, and then her gaze traveled from his bare chest, down his pajama pants, to his bare feet. His skin tingled everywhere she looked, as surely as if she'd dragged her palms down his chest.

"Who the hell are you?" she demanded.

"I should be asking you that question. I live here, not this Calvin person you're looking for. You have the wrong address."

She smirked. "Nice try. I know he doesn't live here, but I know he's here with that bitch." She then lifted a baseball bat he hadn't seen through the peephole, over her right shoulder, as if she were standing at the plate ready to swing.

Anton's hands lifted in defense. "Whoa, hold on. There's no Calvin here, and I don't know who the bitch—I mean, woman—is that you're looking for."

One sculpted brow lifted above her skeptical dark eyes. Despite the volatile situation, he couldn't help appraising her features. When was the last time he'd seen anyone quite so... stunning? With a round face, high cheekbones, and catlike eyes that glared at him but managed to look sensuous at the same time. Her nose tilted slightly upward at the tip, and her full, thick lips could be too much on the wrong face, but settled on hers in a way that drew the eye and made him temporarily forget the damage she could do with that bat nestled on her shoulder.

She wore a red top that, well... it was rather revealing, exposing her midriff and showing off the dark walnut of her flat stomach and the white-gold belly ring nested in her navel. And she obviously wasn't wearing a bra, her large breasts sitting freely on her chest, nipples evident against the soft cotton. He had to force himself to look at her face and keep his gaze there, which wasn't an easy task.

Anton swallowed hard to beat back the lust that reared its horny head as he admired nature's handiwork.

"Sure you don't know them. Unless you want some of this"—she waved the bat—"I suggest you get out of my way and let me handle my business."

"This is *my* apartment," Anton insisted.

These gated communities weren't worth the money. Why pay extra when it was so easy for crazy people to slip in behind someone else, like this psycho obviously had?

"Calvin!" the stranger screamed. When she tried to shove past him, Anton slammed his hand on the doorframe.

"Listen," he said, lowering his voice to a lethal level, "I don't need you waking up my neighbors and causing me problems, all right? This is my apartment. I'm not telling you again. There is no Calvin here. This is 2516 Hargrove Street Apt C. *You have the wrong address.*"

Bad enough she'd woken him up out of bed after a long week, but now she was getting on his nerves with her insistence of trying to get past him to find this Calvin dude.

"No, I do not have the wrong address. Tell me this, do you know who Melissa is?"

Shock jolted Anton's back ramrod straight. "Melissa?"

The stranger smirked knowingly. "You *do* know her. Where is she? Tell her I want to talk." She tapped the bat in her left palm, looking like anything but someone who only wanted to talk.

"Melissa's on a business trip," Anton said, his interest piqued. She'd left for California the day before.

"Is that what she told you?"

He didn't like the direction this conversation was taking. "Who are you and why do you need to speak to my girlfriend?"

Her mouth fell open, and she slowly lowered the bat. "Melissa is your girlfriend?"

"Yes."

"Calvin is my boyfriend. We definitely need to talk."

She stepped forward, trying to gain entrance to the apartment again, but Anton shifted his body and blocked her. They bumped chests, and the stranger bounced back, but not before he experienced the fullness of her soft breasts and caught the scent she wore. Something floral and sweet that made his nostrils flare.

"Excuse me," he muttered, his voice coming out oddly hoarse.

She appeared startled and took an extra step back from him.

An awkward silence descended between them, his arms and neck prickling, as if the hairs there were standing on edge.

Anton barred the door with his arm again. "I'm not letting you into my apartment until you tell me who you are and what the heck your boyfriend has to do with my girlfriend."

"Do I have to explain outside?"

He eyed her with suspicion, still unsure she could be trusted. Unless she knew some kind of martial arts, he was pretty sure he could take her. At the very least, she needed to give up the bat.

"Leave that out here," he said, pointing.

She hesitated, eyeing him with distrust.

"You're the one who showed up at my house talking crazy, and now you want to come inside. If you do, you need the leave the weapon behind. I don't want you tearing me or my shit up."

"I wouldn't do that. I only want a piece of Calvin."

"And Melissa, apparently."

"Maybe. I haven't decided yet." She shrugged, as if threatening assault was no big deal, and set the bat outside the door. Resting her hands on her hips, she said, "There. Satisfied?"

He didn't answer but let her into the apartment and took the liberty of checking her out from behind. The tight-fitting jeans fit low on her hips and snug on her thighs, and her backside looked nice and plump. Meanwhile, the cotton top looked like it had been seared into her skin, it was so tight. If he wasn't already taken, and she wasn't crazy, he might be tempted...

The stranger swung around to face him. "Nice place. Where do you want me?"

What a loaded question.

"Right there." Anton pointed to the sofa. "Have a seat. I'll change real quick. Don't move."

"Don't worry. You're gonna want to hear this." She sat down and crossed her legs.

He didn't like the sound of that and had his suspicions about where the conversation was going, but held his tongue. "What's your name, by the way?"

She angled her head to look up at him. "Tamika. Tamika Jones."

"All right, Tamika. I'm Anton Bevins. I'll be right back."

He exited the room and changed into navy blue sweat pants and a washed-out, red T-shirt from a team-building exercise with the name of the law firm where he worked—Abraham, MacKenzie & Wong—printed on the front.

He returned to the living room, and Tamika was on her feet looking at the collage of photos on the wall above the sofa. Most were family pictures, but there were also some with friends.

"You have a twin brother," she remarked, staring at a photo of him and his brother, arms around each other, grinning hard as they ate popsicles outside the house they grew up in, in Wisconsin.

He remembered that day like it was yesterday. One of the best days of his life. The sun was shining and life was good. At the time, he'd believed with the naïveté of a typical nine-year-old that nothing would change, and he'd always have his brother.

Pain arched into his throat. "Had a twin brother," he corrected huskily.

Tamika swung to face him, and Anton cleared his throat. She opened her mouth to speak, but he cut off whatever question she was about to ask.

"What do you have to tell me about Melissa and your boyfriend?"

Planting her hands on her hips, she replied, "You're not going to like this, but I think your girlfriend and my boyfriend ran off together."

Anton crossed his arms. "I told you, Melissa's on a business trip."

She shook her head vehemently. "She lied. Calvin's gone, and now you're telling me she's gone, too, and I know for a fact they've been seeing each other."

"What proof do you have?" Calvin asked.

"Text messages, plus one day I followed him and saw them holding hands at a restaurant, but I only saw the back of her head."

Stunned, Anton didn't speak for a moment. Maybe he hadn't heard her right. "Holding hands?"

Tamika nodded. "That's right. Your girl might be on a trip, but it's not business related. Calvin told me he was leaving on a weeklong guys' trip, but he took way too many clothes for seven days. And he emptied my bank account."

"Hold up, he stole from you?" This story was getting wilder by the second.

"Yes. He took everything—almost ten thousand dollars. Thanks to him and your girlfriend, I don't have any money. I-I'm broke!" Her voice cracked.

Then, as if the gravity of the situation hit her all at once, tears filled Tamika's eyes and her face crumpled. She dropped to the sofa, burying her head in her hands as she sobbed out loud.

Tamika couldn't believe she'd broken down in front of him. A complete stranger. Like a weakling.

"Here you go," Anton said.

She took the glass of water he extended. "Thank you." Sipping self-consciously, she looked everywhere but at him as he settled in the armchair across from her.

"I'm sorry this happened to you. To find out that your boyfriend's cheating on you and that he stole all your money must be devastating."

"That's an understatement." Tamika cradled the cool glass in both hands. "But I knew he'd been cheating on me for a while. I didn't know he'd run off with my savings, though." She gulped down the last of the water before taking a deep breath and finally looking at Anton across the glass coffee table.

At least he didn't seem as irritated as before. The frown was temporarily gone, and she warmed to the sympathy in his eyes, and thankfully her nipples had stopped tingling from the brief contact at the door.

Anton Bevins was handsome, bordering on pretty. Pretty-handsome. He had the kind of face that made you do stupid shit, like cancel plans with your girlfriends when he called last minute.

Tall, with light-brown eyes, he made her temporarily forget the reason she'd shown up on his doorstep at this god-awful hour in the morning. With thick eyebrows, a light-brown complexion, and serious eyes that didn't flinch or avert when their gazes met, his direct stare made her insides quiver in an odd way. His hair was cut low, and his sturdy jawline accentuated by a goatee and mustache. She regretted he'd covered up his tight body, which consisted of a sculpted chest that tapered to a lean waist, and abs that could star in ab-crunching infomercials on late night television.

A quick perusal of his place when she was alone had shown that he was the neat and orderly type. Even the photos on the wall, which initially seemed like a haphazard collage, were put together in a sequence that commemorated fun times and special occasions like birthdays and graduation in an obviously chronological order based on his age progression in the photos. She didn't see any that looked like they might include Melissa. She'd hoped to finally see the bitch's face.

"How did you find out that Melissa and Calvin are together?" Anton asked. The frown was back.

"A few months ago he started acting weird. Suspicious, really. He started walking out of the room to take calls, and he didn't leave his phone lying around like he used to. One night he came home smelling like perfume and swore that it was one of his clients —he's a graphic designer—who'd hugged him after he took her out for a congratulatory dinner. Of course I didn't buy that bull shit, so I figured out his password. It's his grandmother's birthdate. Throw in a random symbol like an ampersand and boom, I got into his phone. I read his texts while he was sleeping one night."

Anton's eyes widened a smidge, but he didn't comment on her sleuthing. "What did the texts say?"

"I learned a lot. One time your girlfriend texted him this address so he could pick her up."

"He came *here*?" Anton asked, incredulous.

"Yes. She said you were working late, so Calvin took her to dinner. I remember that night, too. I make cosmetics and was working late on some packages that had to go out the next day. Instead of helping me, he ran off with her to dinner." Tamika crossed her arms, fuming at the memory. "Of course I didn't know that at the time. Mostly they sexted each other—talking about times they'd spent together, how much they enjoyed it, using eggplant emojis, et cetera, et cetera. She also sent him pictures of herself in lingerie—and without. Never her face, though."

For a split second, Anton looked startled. Knowing his girlfriend had sent sexy photos to another man must be shocking and painful. Heck, she'd been shocked to see them.

"He used the same combination of numbers and symbols with his grandmother's name as the password for his computer and I logged in there, too, to see what I could find out. I checked his emails, but they're mostly work-related, a few from friends, and spam. I didn't find airline ticket confirmations or any information to tell me where they went."

Anton sat back in the armchair. "You're good. I don't know if I should be impressed or scared."

With a self-satisfied smirk, Tamika said, "Be impressed. Anyway, Calvin left for his guy's trip yesterday, so I decided I would move out while he was gone. But when I checked my bank account, it was empty. He wiped me out!"

She still couldn't believe he'd done that. Cheating was one thing, but stealing her money? And he knew how hard she'd worked and saved for that cash, too. He'd encouraged her to move in with him to save money. The bastard!

Anton shook his head in disbelief. "So, what are you going to do next?"

Tamika shrugged. "Kill him."

"No, seriously."

She stared at him.

Anton let out a little laugh. "You can't kill him. You know that, right?"

"He would deserve it, don't you think?"

"That's beside the point."

"If you saw the screenshots I took, you might feel differently."

He paused, considering her offer, then shook his head. "I don't care."

She didn't blame him. She halfway wished she could unsee the damning evidence. "I'm sorry for all the trouble I caused coming here. Today is not going as planned." She thought she could sneak away from her lying, cheating boyfriend. Instead, he'd thrown a monkey wrench in her plans.

"Today isn't going as planned for me, either," Anton muttered.

She looked up at him, and they both laughed, relieving the tension in the room.

"Did you know... about your girlfriend cheating on you?" Tamika asked tentatively. "I mean, you didn't seem hurt when I told you about her and Calvin. You barely seemed surprised."

Anton sighed and rubbed the back of his head. "Honestly, I wondered if there was something wrong. We've been... off for a while and were supposed to have a talk when she came back from her business trip."

"How long is a while?"

"A couple months at least. She's definitely been different. I guess in the same way you knew Calvin was different."

"You're not hurt?"

"My pride is hurt, and I'm pissed, but our relationship had run its course."

"I had no clue, at first, what was going on with Calvin. We've had our issues, but I've been busy trying to grow my cosmetics business. It's hard work, and when I'm stressed, I can be... a lot."

"You don't say."

"Hey!"

They both laughed again.

"Where did your guy say he was off to?"

"Camping. He loves the outdoors, which is why it didn't seem strange that he was going off into the woods with his friends. I'm not much for camping and all that, so it never bothered me that he went with his friends every now and again. He had his alone time with his boys, and I'd have my alone time with my girls."

Silence, as they both sat with their own thoughts.

"Well, since you said I can't kill him..." Tamika lifted one eyebrow as if to test his resolve on that point.

"No, you can't kill him," Anton confirmed. "And for the record, coming over here with a baseball bat was not wise. If he were here and you attacked him, you'd end up in jail, and then he not only wins, you'll lose big time. You think you're out of money now, wait until you add bail and lawyer fees. Trust me, I know. I'm an attorney."

"You're an attorney? Give me some legal advice! I can't let him get away with this. I can press charges, right?"

"Absolutely. Do you know how he was able to empty your account? Did he steal your password or forge a check—"

"No, he probably walked into the bank and had them give him all the money."

"They wouldn't simply give him all the money..." Anton's eyes narrowed. "Was this a joint account?"

Tamika nodded. "Calvin suggested we get on each other's account in case something happened to one of us. I think he must have another account somewhere that I don't know about, though, because he works every day and has money, but there's only thirty dollars in that account right now."

"If he was a signatory on the account, there's nothing you can do," Anton said quietly.

She knew that, but hearing the words was like a punch in the gut. She'd hoped he would tell her about some obscure law that would allow her to nail Calvin.

"But it was my money!" she exclaimed.

"That's not the way the law sees it. He had a legal right to that account, which means he could take the money."

Tamika jumped to her feet. He was saying things she didn't want to hear. There had to be some recourse. She was going to use that money to pay for marketing and expand her business.

"Are you a criminal attorney?" she asked.

"No. I'm a corporate attorney."

"Then maybe you don't know what you're talking about."

Anton came slowly to his feet. "Actually—"

"I don't want to hear anything else you have to say. You're wrong."

"Tamika, look, I don't know you, but I don't want to see you do something that will end in disappointment. Your best recourse is to talk to Calvin and see if he'll give you the money back. Anything else, you're asking for trouble."

"Thank you for your advice. I'll make my own decisions, like I'm sure you'll make your own about Melissa." She headed to the door.

"Tamika, wait."

Picking up her pace, she ignored him. She had to get out of there. She needed to escape from his pitying looks and deal with this anger that had overtaken her brain. She would cut up all of Calvin's clothes. Burn all his shit. Empty his account of the thirty lousy dollars he had in there and then start looking for the secret account he clearly had hidden from her.

"Tamika, what are you about to do?"

She yanked open the door as more tears filled her eyes. "Don't worry about me," she said breezily over her shoulder.

She couldn't tell her father because she'd get a lecture, and he'd tell her to come home to Augusta. She was twenty-nine years old, but her father insisted on treating her like a child more often than not. She wanted to live her own life and learn from her own mistakes. She didn't want to go back to living under his roof. And she didn't want to hear *I told you so* because he'd never liked Calvin and didn't approve of them moving in together.

Why couldn't she be more like her sister? Camela had been smart and driven. Tamika was a screw up.

She ran down the three steps in front of the apartment and hopped in her car. She didn't look back once as she sped across the parking lot and out the gate.

❧ 3 ❧

With the phone squeezed between her ear and shoulder, Tamika flitted around the bedroom, tossing her personal belongings into boxes. She'd had every intention of cutting up and burning Calvin's clothes and shoes, his precious football trophies, and anything else she could get her hands on, but her friend Layla had talked her out of taking such drastic action.

"Where are you going to go?" Layla asked.

She was one of Tamika's best friends. The other member of their trio was Dana. The three had been best friends ever since they met playing softball in an all-female league. Though they no longer played ball, they remained friends, their different personalities balancing out the friendship circle.

"I haven't figured that part out yet."

Not only was she broke, the landlord had stuck an eviction notice on the door this morning. Apparently, Calvin hadn't paid rent in the last two months, though she'd given him her share. There was no way she could catch up the rent on her own, and even if she did, she couldn't afford the one-bedroom apartment by herself. She wished she could. The neighborhood was nice and the apartment was a nice size. Calvin—who had been using the dining room as an office for his graphic design business—had allotted half of the room as a makeshift warehouse, where she sometimes put together shipments for her cosmetics company, TamCam Cosmetics.

The name was a combination of the first three letters of her name and the first three letters of her older sister's name. Camela had been smart and would have been a great doctor if life were fair and good people didn't die too young.

"You can stay with me, if you like," Layla offered.

"You live in a one-bedroom loft, Layla." Tamika folded two coats in half and dropped them on the pile.

"But it's huge, and I'm hardly ever there. I'm usually at Elijah's. Come stay with me, at least until you figure out what you want to do and where to go."

The offer was tempting, but Tamika was hesitant to inconvenience her friend. Suddenly bone-tired, she dropped her butt onto the bed. "I'm thinking about going back home."

That was the last thing she wanted to do but didn't see any other way. At least her father would be happy.

She'd moved from Augusta, Georgia with big dreams, landing an entry-level chemist position in a lab for a contract manufacturer that developed hair care and cosmetics products for large firms. But she quit after a year when she learned they unethically sourced ingredients and misled their clients about the efficacy of their products.

Venturing out on her own meant she could control the development of the cosmetics she created, from the sourcing to the packaging. She proudly labeled her products cruelty-free, and the ingredients list displayed her commitment to using all-natural and organic raw materials. But her cosmetics line hadn't taken off the way she'd hoped, and her romantic life was completely dead now. Calvin had done more than hurt her. He'd crippled her financially. She didn't have a moment to breathe to get her bearings.

"I know you don't want to do that."

"What choice do I have? I'm obviously too stupid to live on my own."

"Stop. You got taken advantage of. That doesn't make you stupid, and if I ever see Calvin again, I'll knock him out myself."

That made Tamika laugh, because Layla was so far from violent, but she was definitely a good and loyal friend.

"I texted him and asked how the camping trip is going. He responded two hours later, and you know what he said? Going great. Best trip yet."

"I hate him."

"Me, too." Tamika strolled out of the bedroom and into the dining room.

Boxes of her products were stacked against one wall under a long work table, and Calvin's desk with a computer and peripherals were against the other wall. The day before he left on his "guys' trip," he'd taken his iMac to the shop, so he'd told her. But he'd left behind his MacBook Pro.

She walked over to his desk and idly picked up a notepad. "Maybe I should take his precious MacBook to the pawn shop."

"Tamika," Layla warned.

Tamika sighed and was about to replace the pad on the desk when words depressed into the paper caught her eyes. "Hang on a second, Layla." She angled the notepad toward the ceiling light and saw the words better.

Calvin was known for writing with a heavy hand, and he'd written so hard on this notepad that though he'd torn off the top sheet, the words were pressed into the pad. She set down the phone and searched the desk for a pencil. There had to be one there somewhere. She pulled open a desk drawer but found only pens and markers.

"Come on," she muttered.

Nothing on the desk. She pulled open another drawer. Nothing in that one, either.

Eyebrow pencil!

She rushed over to her boxes and tore open a shrink-wrapped

box filled with makeup from one of her Weekend Slumber Party kits, a bestseller. She removed the pencil and then went back over to Calvin's desk.

Carefully, she ran the pencil over the paper, and the words appeared as if by magic. She gasped.

Snatching up the phone, she said, "Hey, I gotta go."

"You okay?" Layla asked in a worried voice.

"Yes. I'll call you later. Bye!"

"Goodb—"

Tamika hung up and stared at the notepad and examined the words. She'd been so upset about what Calvin had done, she hadn't considered that maybe there were clues to his whereabouts here. She yanked open the two desk drawers again and started rummaging through the contents. Nothing but Post-it notes, rubber bands, paper clips—the usual office items. There had to be more information here somewhere.

Tamika paused her frenzied searching. Placing a fist on one hip, she tapped her foot. "If I were a lying, cheating scumbag, where would I hide information?"

She went into the bedroom and yanked clothes and boxes from the top of the closet and tossed his clothes in the dresser onto the floor. She found an envelope with sixty dollars cash, which she pocketed, and kept searching.

The doorbell rang while she was looking under the bed. Her head popped up, and she waited, listening to see if they'd ring again or go away. A few seconds later, the person knocked, but she decided to ignore them and pulled two shoeboxes from under the bed. Flinging them open, she found only tennis shoes inside.

"Dang it," she muttered, disgusted.

The knocking started again and broke her concentration. She jumped up and exited the bedroom. Marching to the door, she yanked it open.

And inhaled.

Anton was standing on the other side, looking tall and elegant in a chocolate suit and shiny black shoes.

"Hey," he said with a smile.

"Hi." She straightened. "What are you doing here?"

He pulled her baseball bat from behind his back. "You forgot this at my apartment."

"Oh." Tamika laughed. She'd been too embarrassed to go back to retrieve it. She frowned. "How did you track me down to get that back to me?"

"You weren't hard to find, and I know people." He shrugged.

"Oh really?"

She was pleasantly surprised he'd gone to so much trouble to give her the bat and had a hard time keeping from grinning, so she didn't bother. She showed all her teeth, and he responded with a little smile that lifted one corner of his mouth.

He was much more reserved than she was, but she liked that. She'd never been attracted to loud mouth men—the ones who burst into parties and whose rowdy antics were part of their persona.

She found Anton's calm and steady composure to be very attractive.

Their eyes locked on each other, and a thrill of excitement scampered down her spine. Something was happening between them, and she wasn't sure what to think. Both he and she were dating cheaters, who were dating each other. Maybe the thrill came from the slight taste of the forbidden.

"Would you like to come in?" Tamika asked.

"Sure."

She took the bat, and Anton stepped over the threshold.

"Can I get you something to drink?" she asked.

"No, I'm good. I haven't had dinner, so I won't stay long."

"Too bad." Disappointment nested in her stomach, but she ignored the sensation.

Anton raised an eyebrow, eyes narrowing ever so slightly.

There it was again, that thing happening between them. A

certain awareness, an attraction that permeated the air and brushed her skin like a whisper.

"I have something to tell you. Guess what I found out?" she asked.

"There's no way I can guess, so you might as well tell me."

"I know where Calvin and Melissa are."

His eyebrows snapped together. "Where?"

"Right here in Atlanta."

4

Tamika's apartment was smaller than Anton's and decorated with mostly black leather furniture and chrome-colored furnishings. He watched her move into the dining room and drop the bat in a corner. This was the first time he'd seen her hair—cut in a Nia Long 90s pixie. Short and sassy, like her.

Swinging around with a flourish, she said, "I'm going to confront him."

"Now wait a minute." Anton lifted his hands to forestall her.

She rushed over, eyes lighting up. "I'm serious. Now that I know he's not in another state or country. He's right here, spending my money on an expensive new apartment. The nerve!"

Anton bit back a laugh. She was so... animated. She looked ready to fight but was so tiny he couldn't imagine her doing much damage to anyone.

"Okay, okay, hold on a minute. Where are they?"

She narrowed her eyes. "Why do you want to know?"

"Because you—we need a plan."

"So you're in?" she asked in an excited voice.

He knew he was going to regret this, but Anton's head bobbed up and down in the affirmative.

Letting out a squeal, Tamika jumped up and down, and her breasts bounced in time to her movements. Anton bit into his bottom lip and tried not to stare—but frankly, they looked perfect and enticing under the tight tank top she wore. He was so enthralled, for a few seconds he completely missed when she stopped moving and was looking at him.

Their gazes met, and she had one of her perfectly arched eyebrows lifted. "See something you like?"

He laughed, half embarrassed but half intrigued. There was something about this woman that he couldn't shake. She would definitely keep him on his toes.

"Yeah, I see something I like."

The air crackled between them, and Tamika swept her tongue between her full lips. The other day her lips had been nude, but today they were coated in a deep wine color that popped against her walnut-toned skin.

"I'm not interested in a rebound thing. In case you haven't noticed, I'm trying to track down my thieving boyfriend and get my money back. If you can help me with that, great. If not..."

Anton took two steps closer and tilted his head. "Are you telling me you don't notice what's happening here?"

"And what do you think is happening, Mr. Bevins?" she asked.

Yeah, she noticed. Her voice was way too husky to pretend otherwise.

"It's Mr. Bevins now?"

"Anton," she corrected.

"We're attracted to each other. Or am I crazy?"

"You're not crazy, but I don't think either of us is in their right mind, do you? We've both been betrayed, me more than you because Calvin not only cheated, he ran off with my money. We probably shouldn't do anything that we'll regret later."

In the silence, Anton weighed her words, reluctant to admit that she was right. He was pushing too hard, too soon, but he was already a little obsessed with her. He hadn't stopped thinking about her since she left his apartment, and bringing by the bat was the only excuse he could think of to see her again.

"You're right, this is an emotional time."

He shouldn't push too hard. She was going through a rough period, and though he was definitely interested, he didn't want her to use him as a rebound or a way to get back at her boyfriend. Whatever happened between him and Tamika needed to happen because they were both of sound mind and lucid thought.

"Let's stay focused on Calvin and Melissa, for now. How do you know they're in Atlanta?"

Tamika returned to the dining room, and his eyes followed her, his body tightening with tension as he watched her move fluidly, confidently, like a woman who knew her own appeal. Picking up a notepad, she held it aloft with a flourish.

Anton stayed in the same spot, not trusting himself to move any closer to her. He wasn't certain that he could keep his hands to himself. "What's that?"

"This is where they are. Midtown Towers. Ever heard of it?"

"Yeah, I once dropped off some documents there for a client on my way home." He ambled over to her, stuffing his hands in his pockets and frowning at the paper she'd rubbed pencil over to highlight the words on the page. In addition to the name of the apartment complex, there was a date, underlined twice, which happened to be last Friday. "How do you know that's where they are?" Anton asked, though he agreed with her suspicions.

"I *don't* know, but these are brand new apartments, and I remember one time Calvin said that he'd like to move to a nicer place. One that's more central where he didn't always have to hop in the car to get something to eat. Not too long ago, he got a lucrative contract with one of the airlines, and a few days later I caught him looking at luxury apartments online that offered concierge services, a yoga studio, a state-of-the-art gym, all that jazz—basically amenities that sound enticing but that most people never really take advantage of. So, I think that's where he is. He and your girl are setting up house in a new luxury apartment."

"Melissa had been wanting us to move to a new place. She thought I should upgrade, considering how much money I made, but I'm not interested in spending more money on an apartment, and I'm satisfied with where I live." Anton paused, thinking. "What you're saying makes sense, but they could be literally anywhere. He might have gone to look at an apartment in Midtown Towers, but that doesn't mean they ended up there."

"Wouldn't you like to find out?"

"So you've given up on the idea that they took a trip somewhere?" Anton asked.

"Calvin took too much of his clothes. It's also suspicious that his computer—the main one he uses for work—happened to need fixing and had to be placed in the shop while he's supposedly out of town. And to be honest, I think I would have seen a confirmation for the trip when I went through his email. He didn't have many unread messages, and what I saw didn't hint at a trip."

"Sounds to me like you're looking for a partner in crime. As you pointed out, Melissa cheated on me, but she didn't take my money."

"Does that mean you're not willing to help me track them down?"

"I'm willing to help you, but here's the thing. You can't run off playing detective, judge, and executioner. It's not sensible. Like I said, I know people. We hire investigators all the time for our clients. Let me get in touch with one of them, and I'll see what we can find out."

"I don't have time to waste. I want to know *now*. I'm going over there."

"To do what?"

"Sit in the lobby and wait."

Anton laughed and shook his head. This woman was nuts. "You might not see them."

"Then I'll knock on every door in the building until I find them," she said, and he believed her.

"You can't be serious."

"I am. He has almost ten thousand dollars of my money. I don't want to call and tip him off. I want to catch the lying turd by surprise." Her eyes flashed with anger.

Anton groaned and ran a hand over his head. He was going to regret this. "You can't go over there alone."

Her eyes lit up. "So you're coming?"

He sighed. "Yes."

Tamika squealed and clapped her hands.

"If we don't see them tonight, I'll check with one of the investigators we use and see what they can find out."

Tamika sighed dramatically. "Thank you."

"I do have one more thing to mention."

"What's that?"

"I don't want you to get the wrong idea."

"And why would I do that, Anton?"

"Because of what I'm going to ask you. But it's strictly platonic. Totally innocent."

"Mhmm. If that's what you want me to think. What did you have in mind?"

He rubbed his stomach. "I'm hungry, and the lobby at Midtown Towers opens into a bar and restaurant. Have you eaten yet?"

"Are you inviting me to dinner?" She batted her lashes.

Anton chuckled. "Maybe."

"Don't be shy now. Shoot your shot."

He found himself smiling. Yeah, he was really digging this woman. She was unlike anyone else he'd ever met, and that was a good thing. She certainly wasn't like some of the women he'd dated in the past, women he met in his line of work or through some networking event. Everyone put on airs, pretending they were more serious than they were because no one wanted a bad reputation in his field.

"If I shoot my shot, we might end up doing something you regret. And when we do something, I don't want you to regret it."

She inhaled slowly, chest lifting up and down. "Okay. So, are you definitely inviting me to dinner or is that still a maybe?"

"I'm inviting you to dinner."

"Then I accept your invitation. Mind giving me a few minutes to change?"

"I don't mind at all."

"I'll be right back."

She spun around and he had the pleasure of watching her plump behind walk away and disappear into a room. Anton took a seat on the leather couch and waited, glancing at his watch to note the time.

Ten minutes later, Tamika returned, and he was hard-pressed to keep his mouth from dropping open. She'd done a lot in ten minutes. Blinking, he stared in admiration at the way the little black dress fit over her curves and flared out to swirl around her knees. Her short black hair was brushed flat on her head and glossy, giving her a sleek, sexy look. Strappy heels with gold rhinestones added height and showed off red-painted toenails, and she'd also put on more makeup, highlighting her eyes and adding bronzer to her cheeks.

"Don't look so surprised, Anton. I know how to dress up every now and again."

"I see," he said, getting to his feet.

"I hope they have strong drinks at this place." Tamika led the way to the door.

"I'm sure they do."

"Good. I'm hungry and I plan to get my drink on." She turned to face him. "I hope you have a high balance on that card."

Laughing, he shook his head. "Don't worry, I got you."

❧ 5 ☙

The doorman, an older guy with a thick mustache and wearing a cap to match his dark blue uniform, greeted Tamika and Anton and held the door open for them as they walked into Madison Towers. Upon entering, Tamika blinked in shock, impressed by the stunning interior. The inside of Madison Towers was definitely luxurious and a huge step up from where she and Calvin currently lived.

Large chandeliers hovered above black tile that covered the floor all the way to the bank of elevators. To the right was the bar and restaurant Anton had mentioned. Soft piano music came through hidden speakers, and a couple of women sipped drinks on stools as they chatted up the buff, good-looking bartender.

"Nice, isn't it?" Anton said.

"Real nice," Tamika murmured.

They stepped off the tile onto the carpeted floor toward one of the empty round tables, each one surrounded by three orange leather chairs that looked more appropriate for a living room than a restaurant dining room. They sat down where they had a good view, close to a window that showed people rushing along to their destinations, and cars filled with commuters cruising by.

Right away, Tamika ordered a lemon drop, and Anton

ordered a Black Russian. They agreed on the appetizer sampler of stuffed mushrooms, salt cod croquettes, and batter-fried cauliflower to start.

When the waitress walked away, Anton loosened his tie. "So, what's the plan? We sit here and wait?"

"That's it. Maybe we'll see them. Maybe we won't." She shrugged, pretending to be unbothered.

"Well, since we have some time to kill, tell me about your cosmetics business."

He faced the lobby, and Tamika sat to his left with her back to the window so she could also keep an eye on the lobby and the bank of elevators.

She sipped her drink, savoring the tart flavor before replacing the cocktail on the table and settling her tush more comfortably in the soft chair. "There's not much to tell. Right now, my business is online and strictly mail order, but it pays the bills. One day I'd like to be in stores and have a distribution deal with Ulta or someplace like that. I started out mixing batches in my own kitchen, but now I rent space in a commercial kitchen."

"How long have you been making cosmetics?"

"For years, mostly as a hobby. Then four years ago I quit my job to devote more time to my products. I took a major leap of faith, and two years ago—finally—I moved from making products in my kitchen to the space I rent. That was scary."

She still remembered the day she signed the lease, the knots in the stomach, the doubts—wondering if she were crazy and moving too fast. Ignoring her father's warnings that maybe she was moving too fast. But by expanding her workspace she could make larger batches of products and store them in a climate-controlled environment.

"Owning my own business hasn't been what I envisioned," she admitted. She couldn't believe she was telling him that. She hadn't told anyone else, including her best friends. She'd been too busy pretending that she loved being an entrepreneur.

"What did you envision?"

"Honestly, I'm not sure, but it's a lot of work, and I don't enjoy most of it."

His eyebrows lifted higher. "That's not the answer I expected."

Her cheeks heated. "I know, but I know my limitations. I'm an idea person, a creative. I love being in the lab, but managing the business sucks, and it's harder than I thought. I don't like having to do everything myself—marketing, financials, et cetera, et cetera, but I can't afford to hire help."

"Or maybe you can't afford to not hire help. That's how you scale up," Anton said.

She'd heard that advice before, but the idea was daunting. "I don't know. I'm not sure I have the ability to turn my company into a multimillion-dollar business. But I want to."

Anton's eyes became thoughtful. "Don't sell yourself short."

"I'm being realistic. And honestly..." Tamika paused. She didn't normally open up so easily to people. She shared almost everything with her best friends, but Anton wasn't a friend. He was more or less a stranger, but he seemed genuinely interested in learning more about her and her business, which encouraged her to divulge more. "The reason I'm in this profession was because of my sister."

There. The truth was out.

He frowned. "She encouraged you to do it?"

Tamika cast her eyes around the large open space at the other people quietly talking at the few occupied tables. She sipped her drink, relishing the lemony flavor before she continued. "No, she—Camela, that's my sister's name—wanted to be a doctor, and I guess you could say that I idolized her. She was pretty and smart. Made all A's, played sports, and was president of the French club, all of that. The perfect student. Anyway, she passed away when I was in high school, when she was a few years into Emory University on a full ride scholarship.

"She got sick one day, but being the hard worker that she was, she continued studying, going to her part-time job, and pushing through. She became so sick, her roommates had to physically carry her to the doctor, but by then it was too late. Respiratory failure, from pneumonia. Can you believe that? A twenty-one-year-old dying of complications from pneumonia." A small burst of pain filled her chest, and Tamika's shoulders drooped.

"Damn, I'm sorry."

"It still hurts, but I'm fine. I was in high school at the time, a full thirteen years ago, and I've had plenty of time to recover. Before that, all I cared about was fashion and looking cute." She laughed.

Anton didn't comment, but his gaze swept her frame, and her bare arms tingled at his silent inspection.

"When Camela passed, I wanted to do something more. I decided I wanted to become a doctor because that's what she wanted, but halfway through undergrad I realized her path wasn't for me. The good news was, I did find out that I enjoyed science and ended up focusing on chemistry."

"Do you feel like you've completely recovered from her death?" Anton asked. The question was asked in a low voice, his light eyes intense.

"Yeah. I mean, it was hard at first for me and my family. Everybody loved Cam, but then it got easier as time went by." She watched him nod and tip the tumbler of dark liquid to his lips. "You know what it's like to lose a sibling though, don't you? Your twin?"

"Yeah." Anton became preoccupied with staring down into the contents of his glass.

She knew that look. She'd seen it many times on her parents' faces after Camela died. The look of avoidance. The look of prolonged grief, not hidden as well as the bearer had hoped.

"How did he die?" she asked.

He laughed, but it was an uncomfortable sound and lacked any humor. He looked ill-at-ease and rubbed his palms up and down his thighs. "That's not why we're here. We're getting too serious." He glanced over at the bar. "Where's that waitress? I'm starving."

"Come on, Anton, I bared my soul to you about my sister. The least you could do is tell me a little something about your brother." Tamika prodded him in a soft voice, careful not to push too hard because she suspected she was dangerously close to crossing a line he didn't want her anywhere near, and that could cause him to shut down completely.

"He died a long time ago—much longer ago than when your sister died." The loss of his brother obviously still pained him deeply. He couldn't even look at her.

"How long ago?" Tamika asked gently.

He groaned and scrubbed a hand back and forth across the top of his head. "You're not going to give up, are you?"

"Nope." She looked him dead in the face.

He let out a sound that came out as a combination of a laugh and sigh. Then, folding his arms on the table, he said in a quiet voice, "He drowned, twenty-two years ago. We were nine, and it happened not long after that picture you saw."

He swallowed and shifted in the chair. Tamika sensed he wanted to say more and remained silent, letting him continue at his own pace.

"A bunch of us were down at the riverbank goofing around. Me, Ricky, our older brother Pat, and some other kids from the neighborhood. We weren't supposed to be there because there weren't any adults, but you know how kids are. Hard-headed. Somehow, Ricky slipped into the water and got pulled along with the current. We'd been horsing around for a while, so he didn't have much fight in him. Plus, he wasn't the best swimmer. He got swept downstream, and the whole time I was running along the bank, trying to keep up, screaming and yelling at him with our older brother and six more kids behind me doing the same. We told him to stay strong, to hang on, but we lost him after a while." A faraway look came into his eyes. "They found his body the next day. I never went back to that spot. Fucking hate being near the water now." His jaw tightened and his gaze dropped to the table.

Tamika let silence envelope them before she spoke again. "I saw my sister die, too," she whispered.

That was the hardest part of her memories. She could handle recalling everything else—the phone call that had them rushing to the hospital, the funeral, and going into Camela's room at home to sit on the bed and reminisce and soak up her energy. But the memory of those last minutes left her painfully raw.

"I was holding her hand in the hospital. Like you did for your brother, I encouraged her to hold on. But... but right before she died, I could almost swear that she said to me, 'I'm ready.' Then she left me. I just sat there and cried." Her voice wobbled.

"I'm sorry." His eyes filled with sympathy and compassion.

"I'm sorry for you, too." Tamika released a heavy breath. "My mom passed around the time I became serious about making my own cosmetics. I started out making tinted lip balm and lipstick and then moved into skincare products, making small batches that I shared with friends and then started selling to friends and friends of friends. When I combined my most popular lip color, lip gloss, and lip liner into a lip kit, sales took off, and I saw the potential for my cosmetics business to do well. My mom was so proud and always encouraged me. 'That's your talent, Tam Tam,' she used to say. She was my best friend. We were like this." She twisted her middle finger around her forefinger. The pain of losing her mother was fresher and expanded in her chest like an inflating balloon.

The waitress's arrival with the appetizers created a break in the heavy conversation. She asked if they were ready to order their meals, but they both shook their heads. When she left, they stared at the platter of food in silence.

Anton was the one who finally spoke. "We have more in common than I realized. More than two people who got cheated on."

Tamika managed to smile. "Yeah, we do."

$$\text{🦋} \quad 6 \quad \text{🦋}$$

After a lull in the conversation, Anton said, "I decided to go to law school because of my brother." He picked up a battered cauliflower with his fingers and popped it in his mouth.

"Really?"

He nodded. "One time for career day, one of our friend's dads came to talk to the class, and he was an attorney. He told us about the different types of attorneys, and Ricky was fascinated by the idea of being an entertainment attorney. He was a cut-up. I guess you could say he was the fun one, and I was the serious one, so I think he imagined himself hanging out with celebrities and famous people. I wasn't sure what I wanted to do. One minute, a fireman, the next minute a truck driver, the next minute a chef."

"Can you cook?" Tamika asked.

"Barely, but I like to eat." He smiled. "Anyway, I was all over the place, but I was only nine, right, so that's to be expected. When Ricky died, I became obsessed with becoming an entertainment lawyer. I was going to do it for Ricky. But once I entered law school, I was more interested in contracts and business structures and all that stuff that would have put Ricky to sleep. After talking with my career counselor, I ended up choosing corporate law. At first, that decision was like a weird betrayal, but after a while, I settled into the idea."

"Because it fit your personality."

"Yeah. Long hours, though. But... I think Ricky would be proud."

Tamika studied him across the table and sympathized with the pain he was experiencing. The lines of his face were drawn. "You don't talk about him much, do you?"

He seemed surprised by her assessment. "No, I don't."

"You should talk about him more," she said gently.

"Why?"

"Because it gets easier the more you do. I promise it does. There was a time when I couldn't talk about my sister at all because it hurt too much, but now I talk about her *all* the time," she said with a little laugh. "Same with my mom."

"And that helped?" He sounded and looked skeptical.

"Yes. People grieve differently, but bottling up the pain won't help you or make the loss any easier. You need to let out your grief. You need to talk about him. Share the memories with people you know." Tamika reached across the table and covered his fist with her hand.

Anton looked in her eyes, and she smiled. After a while, he smiled back, and that initial attraction she'd experienced with him came flooding back tenfold. She should only be thinking about helping him through the painful memories, but that smile made her notice once again how good-looking he was. The sharp line of his jaw and intense eyes softened, making her stomach contract reflexively as her nipples tightened.

She wondered what he was like in bed. In her experience, quiet men were extremely dangerous. They were the ones who'd have you fiending for them all hours of the day and night. They didn't brag about their sexual prowess because they didn't need to. They simply put in the work and let their actions speak louder than words ever could.

"Thanks," Anton said.

There was nothing inappropriate about his voice, yet heat sizzled across her skin. She imagined a dark room and a soft bed, him whispering to her in that same velvety soft voice, but more guttural. The somber conversation topic kept her on her best behavior, but if they were in a different location at a different time, she'd be on her way to unleashing her inner slut.

Tamika removed her hand from his and shifted in the chair. "You're welcome."

Anton opened his mouth as if to speak, but his gaze flicked to the lobby and he stiffened. Tamika twisted her head and followed his gaze. Her mouth fell open.

Calvin was at the elevator, wearing a tan jacket and tan slacks that posed a striking contrast to his mahogany skin. His arm was casually thrown around the shoulders of an attractive woman with peachy-brown skin and a long sheath of shiny hair cascading down her back, as if she'd stepped out of a shampoo commercial minutes before. She wore a cute red dress that hugged her shapely body. They looked like they were returning from a date.

"That's Melissa," she heard Anton murmur in shock, as if—despite their previous conversations—he only now fully understood that his girlfriend had run off with another man.

Tamika had thought coming here was a long shot, but they'd made the right decision. She hopped up from her chair and tossed her little black purse over her shoulder.

"Tamika, wait."

Anton grabbed her wrist, but she easily snatched her arm free and charged toward the couple. All the fury from the past week thundered through her like a runaway train.

"Calvin!" she screamed.

The doorman, Calvin, and Melissa turned in her direction, and Calvin's eyes widened when he saw her.

"You lying, thieving..." Claws out, Tamika was ready to

attack, but Anton grabbed her around the waist from behind and pulled her tight against his body.

"Calm down," he whispered, breath brushing her neck.

The air contracted and for a few moments, time stood still as Tamika lost her ability to think. All she could do was *feel*. Her mind zeroed in on the warmth at her back, the firmness of Anton's body, and the way the spot between her thighs pulsed at the weight of his arm around her waist. Being held against him was eye-opening, and Tamika temporarily forgot her anger, flustered by her visceral reaction to their close contact.

"Anton, what are you doing here?" Melissa asked, staring at him.

Anger leaked from Tamika's muscles, and she relaxed her tense body.

Anton released her and stood beside her, facing the couple. "Shouldn't I be asking you that question, since you told me you were on a business trip in California?"

"I..."

Calvin dropped his arm from around Melissa. "I don't know what's going on here, but—"

Tamika planted her hands on her hips. "You know exactly what's going on. You're busted, liar. You said you were on a trip with the boys, but instead I find you here. This is an apartment complex, Calvin. Do you care to explain?"

"Listen, I know how it looks."

"It looks like the two of you are having an affair behind our backs," Tamika snapped.

Calvin and Melissa shared a guilty glance, and then Melissa looked at Anton, her eyes imploring. "I didn't mean for this to happen. I didn't know how to tell you."

"So you ran off and pretended you were going on a trip? How exactly did you intend to explain what was happening when you came back from your so-called trip to California?" Anton folded his arms across his chest.

"I don't... I don't know. I didn't think that far ahead." Melissa swallowed and looked at Calvin for help.

He immediately straightened his shoulders and placed a protective arm around her. The move did two things—angered Tamika and hurt her immensely. Here was the man she thought cared about her, blatantly showing that the woman he really cared about was standing beside him.

"We didn't mean for this to happen, but now that you know..." He paused as the elevator doors opened and a group of four exited and walked around them. "Now that you know, I see this as a good thing. We didn't want to lie, but we didn't know what else to do. We—"

"You could have told the truth," Tamika hissed between clenched teeth. "You could have been upfront and honest instead of sneaking around behind our backs."

Calvin glared at her. "How did you find out about us? How did you find out we were here?"

"Wouldn't you like to know?" Tamika smirked.

"Yes, I would. That's why I asked," Calvin said louder, almost to the point of yelling.

"Watch your damn mouth talking to her," Anton said, moving closer to Tamika.

Having him back her up, in the face of Calvin protecting Melissa, bolstered Tamika's confidence.

Tilting up her chin, she said, "Because you're sloppy, Calvin. I saw the texts the two of you exchanged, and I have screen shots in case you want to deny that you were sending dirty texts to each other."

Melissa lowered her gaze to the black tile.

Calvin's arm dropped from her shoulders again, and his eyebrows snapped low over his eyes. "You went through my phone?"

"Yes!"

"You had no right to invade my privacy."

"And you had no right to steal from me!" Tamika yelled, her

voice quivering.

Melissa lifted her gaze and shot Calvin a questioning glance. "What is she talking about?"

"All the money for your little move came from me. He emptied my bank account."

"Is that true?" Melissa asked, aghast.

"No, that's not true," Calvin replied, keeping his eyes on Tamika. "That was *our* bank account. *Our* money."

"*My* money," Tamika insisted, tapping her chest with her thumb. "Your name was on the account, but every dollar in there belonged to *me*. You stole almost ten thousand dollars from me, that you know I needed for my business. I want every dime of it back."

"Well you're not getting it back. I used *our* money to start a new life."

"He didn't pay the last two months' rent, either, by the way," Tamika said to Melissa. "I gave him my half, but he obviously pocketed it. So guess who got an eviction notice today? Me! Now I have nowhere to go." Tears of anger and frustration filled her eyes, but she blinked them back.

I will not cry in front of him. I will not cry in front of him.

The doorman walked up. "Excuse me, I'm going to need you to keep your voices down or take this conversation elsewhere," he said in a hushed voice.

Calvin glared at her in disgust. "You see, Tamika, this is why I had to leave, because you're too damn loud. Too annoying. You make me—"

Anton snatched Calvin by the collar and yanked him up on his toes so their faces were only inches apart. Melissa gasped, eyes widening, and Tamika took a surprised step back.

"Hey!" the doorman said, raising a hand to calm the tension, but he wasn't foolish enough to step between them. He looked around nervously for help.

Anton spoke softly to Calvin, but his voice was filled with menace. "Shut the fuck up."

❧ 7 ❧

Anton didn't know what came over him. All he knew was that Tamika didn't deserve to be talked to in that way, and he couldn't stand idly by and allow it.

One minute he was listening to Calvin rant, the next he had fisted Calvin's jacket lapels in his hands and was itching for a fight. He wasn't a violent person, and the last time he remembered throwing fists was in high school. In fact, his calm and cool was considered one of his positive traits, and at the firm they called him the Silent Dragon. He didn't huff and puff like some of the other attorneys, but he got the job done, saving the fire-breathing for only when absolutely necessary.

Two seconds ago had been absolutely necessary. He could no longer stand there while that piece of shit Calvin tried to embarrass Tamika when he was in the wrong.

Anton's eyes bored into Calvin's to make sure the other man understood that he meant business when he spoke. "When you open your mouth again, watch your tone. You're not going to talk to Tamika like that anymore. You're going to treat her with the respect she deserves because you're the one in the wrong, you're the one that had no business stealing from her, and you're the one who had no right to stop paying the rent when she was giving you her half. You're a piece of shit. You're a cheat and a thief. Now, we're going to continue this conversation, and you're going to check your tone and your attitude with her moving forward. We clear?"

Calvin's jaw firmed. "Yeah, we're clear," he muttered.

Anton released him and both men stepped back slowly from each other. Anton sensed Tamika's eyes on him, but he didn't look at her immediately. He kept his eyes on Calvin, who was making a big show of straightening his wrinkled jacket.

"I've never seen you behave like that," Melissa remarked, her voice filled with wonder.

Sickened by her lies, Anton held back a sneer. She was looking at him as if he were a stranger, but if anyone was a stranger, she was. She'd done him a favor by leaving, actually, because he'd intended to end their relationship, though not in such a spectacular way. The only reason he was here was because of Tamika, and the sooner he and Melissa cut ties, the better.

"I need you to come get your shit within the next forty-eight hours or I'm putting everything by the dumpster," he said. Legally, he didn't have the right to do that, but he knew she would not ignore his threat.

She dropped her gaze and clutched her purse closer to her side.

"You need to come get your things, too," Tamika said to Calvin.

"I was planning to. I'll be there tomorrow."

"Call first."

His eyes narrowed. "I'll do that."

"And I want my money."

"I can't help you with that," Calvin said dismissively.

"He's a lawyer," Melissa said in a low voice.

Surprise and a hint of fear filled Calvin's eyes.

Anton smiled. "That's right. If I were you, I'd find a way to pay her back for the money you took from her savings account."

"But I don't have all that money anymore!" Calvin exclaimed.

"I'm sure she'll accept a payment plan. You'll accept weekly or monthly installments, won't you, Tamika?" He looked down at her.

She stood taller. Smiling, she replied, "I sure will. Whatever you think is best, counselor."

"I'll draft a contract and terms and have them delivered to you next week," Anton told Calvin.

"You can send all correspondence to my business address," Tamika added.

Calvin's gaze shifted between them. "What's going on? Are the two of you together now?"

"Worry about yourself. Just come get your shit," Tamika said.

Calvin's lips tightened, and he clearly wanted to make a scathing remark, but one glance at Anton and the mental shift he made was obvious.

The elevator dinged open again, and Calvin took Melissa's hand. "We'll be in touch."

He dragged her along with him, and they almost ran over the couple exiting the cabin.

After watching the doors close, Anton turned away and made direct eye contact with the doorman, who still stood nearby. Anton had completely forgotten about him.

"Did you lose something?" he asked.

The older man started, cleared his throat, and scampered away.

"I need to pay the bill. Then we'll go somewhere else to eat," Anton said to Tamika.

She shook her head. "I don't think I can eat anything right now, and I don't want to go anywhere else. Would you take me home?"

The bluster from a few minutes ago was gone. She looked deflated. Drained of all her sparkle.

"Sure, I can do that."

They went back to the restaurant, and he paid the tab and asked the waitress to box up the food.

"This is yours. You can eat it later if you want," he said, as they walked toward the door.

The doorman opened the door, and they exited into the balmy night air, Tamika walking ahead of him.

"Tamika." Anton took her wrist, fingers curling around her soft, smooth skin. She stopped and faced him. "I know you have a lot on your mind right now, but if you need a place to stay, you can stay at my apartment after Melissa moves out." He'd considered making her that offer when she said she had nowhere to go. He wished he could kick Calvin's ass for putting her in that position.

"Didn't you hear? I'm too loud. You don't want me in your place. I'll be fine." She tugged away her hand and continued walking.

Anton followed more slowly with the box of food in his hand. Tamika had friends and family and probably would be fine. After all, she'd lived twenty-nine years without him in her life, but while he wasn't responsible for her, he sure felt like he was. Hell, they'd bonded over shared pain and the unfortunate experience of cheating significant others. He was closer to her than he'd been to anyone else in a long time.

He opened the car door, and she slid in, crossing one leg over the other. He shouldn't, but his eyes lingered over the expanse of exposed thigh and toned calves. Cursing softly to himself, he shut the door.

What the hell was wrong with him? This woman had him acting all outside of his character. First, she had him behaving like a member of the Scooby Doo gang trying to solve a crime, staking out the lobby of a high-end apartment building to catch their cheating exes. Second, he'd almost gotten into a fist fight. Third, he was checking out her shapely legs when he should be acting more sympathetic because of her predicament.

They drove in silence all the way back to her apartment. She didn't look at him the entire time, her gaze focused on the passing nighttime scenery. Every now and again he glanced at her, noting the slumped shoulders and the way she'd wrapped her arms around her torso protectively. He wanted to wrap his arms around her and shield her from the pain and misery Calvin and Melissa had caused, but he figured she wasn't in the right frame of mind to accept such an outward display of compassion.

When they arrived at her apartment, he parked in front of the unit and they sat in the car, neither saying a word. That lasted for a few minutes until Tamika finally spoke.

"I don't want to go inside. I feel like I've lost everything. I hate him so much." Her voice sounded low and hoarse, as if she had been crying.

Anton's eyes swept over her downcast eyes and downturned lips. "I meant what I said. You can come stay with me until you get back on your feet. Melissa wasn't paying rent, and you don't have to, either."

"She must've helped in some way, though, right? You need money for bills or something."

"She bought groceries every now and again. If you want to do that, that's fine. But I make a really good salary and I don't need help. Meanwhile, you need to replenish your lost funds so you can keep your business afloat. If you really have nowhere else to go, this is an offer of help, until you can get back on your feet."

She smiled at him. "You're something else, Anton. Melissa realizes it too, you know. I saw the look on her face after you grabbed Calvin. She knows she made a mistake."

"That was shock. I don't think she's ever seen me angry."

"No way. After she heard what I said about Calvin and saw you grab him to defend me, that woman was rethinking her options. She probably would have jumped your bones if we weren't all standing there in public. Believe me. And I don't blame her." She emphasized the last two sentences in a way that caught his attention—suggesting she'd had the same thoughts as Melissa.

Tamika exited the vehicle and Anton followed. At the door, he handed her the box of food.

A faint smile touched her lips. "Thanks. I'm actually glad you took the food because I am sort of hungry."

"I figured," he said, smiling in return.

She huffed out a breath. "What about you? You haven't eaten."

"I'll pick up something on the way home. Pizza, maybe."

"Well... if you don't have anywhere to go, you're welcome to come in and chat for a little bit. And you could help me eat this food." She held up the box.

"That's not going to fill me up. How about we start with that as an appetizer, and we order a pizza?"

"You, sir, have a deal."

Tamika opened the door and Anton followed her in. As soon as he stepped across the threshold, something came over him, a pressure in his chest and thighs. A pressure that suggested something huge was about to happen.

He shut the door quietly behind him.

8

Tamika handed Anton his second beer of the night and joined him on the floor with the open box of pizza. The first time she'd handed him a bottle of the locally made craft beer, she'd told him to drink up because it was Calvin's favorite.

After laughing at her vindictiveness, they devoured the appetizers from Madison Towers, both much hungrier than they'd realized.

He was completely relaxed, his jacket hanging over the arm of the sofa, tie removed, and his shirtsleeves rolled up. Tamika had removed her shoes but still wore the little black dress.

Anton idly examined the dark, heavy-looking furniture and figured Calvin and Melissa had no intention of taking any of the items to Madison Towers. Melissa was very particular about her decorating expectations. Anton's apartment hadn't been up to par, so he figured Calvin would leave everything behind for Tamika and buy all new pieces for the new place. That meant he'd have to—if he hadn't already—furnish the new apartment with high-end pieces, pay the deposit and first month's rent on the luxury apartment, and wine and dine Melissa on a regular basis. No wonder the guy had stolen Tamika's money.

Tamika placed two slices of pizza on her plate and lifted a third to her mouth. "Mmm, so good," she mumbled around the food, sighing with satisfaction.

"You can't go wrong with pepperoni and extra cheese," Anton said, folding a slice and shoving a large portion into his mouth.

Still chewing, Tamika looked at him with an impish light in her dark eyes.

"Uh-oh," Anton said.

She laughed. After what happened tonight, it was good to see she hadn't completely disappeared behind a curtain of despair.

"I want to ask you something," she said.

"Go ahead."

Gearing up, she crossed her legs and resettled on the floor. "Tell me a deep dark secret about yourself. It's got to be something juicy."

"So you can blackmail me? No way." Anton shook his head and continued eating.

"Oh, come on! We're bonding, aren't we? Two heartbroken souls, neither of whom want to face the reality of our empty apartments."

If that's why she thought he was there, she was dead wrong. He had no problem being alone in that apartment and welcomed the solitude without Melissa and her nitpicking around.

He was still there because he'd decided to sleep with Tamika. He should be ashamed of himself, but the urge to fuck her was eating him alive and paced inside him like a hungry lion, stalking its prey. Tamika was the prey. She just didn't know it yet.

"Tell me a secret, Anton. I promise not to tell anyone."

Resting his arm on the sofa, he studied her across the pizza box, contemplating what to share. "Okay, I'll tell you a secret, but if you tell anyone, I'm kicking your ass."

"I won't," she insisted, giggling.

She had the most girly laugh. One that tightened his stomach and made him want to grab her by the back of the neck and kiss her red-tinted lips.

"This happened when I was fourteen. Young and dumb."

"Weren't we all, at some point," Tamika interjected.

"I stole my dad's car and went for a joy ride."

"*Noooo.*" Her mouth fell open.

Anton nodded but kept talking. "That's not the worst of it. Of course my dumb ass ended up in an accident. I ran into the front of a store trying not to hit a dog that ran across the street. The place was closed at the time, but I went right through the front and into the display case. I ran to a house nearby, the owner let me use his phone, and I called my older brother at his girl's house. Pat—Patrick—is three years older than me. He met me over there and took the blame for the accident, pretended he was the one who'd taken the car without permission and crashed. My dad was furious. Cops showed up. The scene was chaotic. Pat was grounded for a month and had to pay for the repairs."

Tamika's mouth was hanging open as he finished the tale. "Well, that was very nice of you to avoid hitting the dog, but taking your father's car at fourteen—that's bad, Anton."

"I know. You don't have to tell me. I look back on that day and wonder what the hell I was thinking about."

"So why did your brother take the fall for you?" She bit into her slice of pizza.

"He said because I was his little brother, and..." His throat went tight. "He couldn't save Ricky, but he wasn't going to let shit happen to me. I was going to become a lawyer, and he didn't want anything to jeopardize that."

Tamika stopped chewing. "Wow," she said quietly, around a mouthful of food.

"Yeah." He'd never forgotten those words or how his brother had taken the fall for him. That day had cemented their bond forever.

"Where's your brother now?"

"He lives in Florida. He's married with two kids and drives trucks for a living."

"Are you still close?"

"Yes."

Tamika picked a piece of pepperoni off the pizza on her plate. "I don't think I can top that," she said demurely.

"Somehow, I doubt that," Anton said dryly. "You definitely have the air of someone who's done some things. You showed up at my house with a baseball bat, remember?"

"True." She laughed. "Okay, *fine*, I do have a story. I was fourteen, same age as you, when I found out my married neighbor, Mrs. Demp, was having an affair with the mailman."

"The mailman? Come on." Anton tipped the bottle of beer to his lips.

"I swear. I took pictures of him entering and leaving the house and started blackmailing her."

Anton coughed and pounded his chest. "I was right about the blackmailing!"

"Hush!" Tamika covered her mouth and giggled again. "I know what I did was awful, but at the time there was this MAC makeup kit that I really wanted. My dad had said no and insisted I could get what I wanted at Wal-Mart, and I better be glad he was letting me wear makeup at fourteen." She rolled her eyes. "I demanded Mrs. Demp buy the kit for me but felt really bad about it afterward. Well, not right after, but a couple of weeks later I did."

"Your parents never questioned how you got the kit?"

"Mrs. Demp told them I'd helped her with some yard work and that was my reward. I'm not entirely sure my parents believed that story, but she was an adult and they didn't have an alternative explanation, which meant they had no choice but to accept what she said." She shrugged.

"Did her husband ever find out about the mailman?"

"Not that I know of, but she found out those long business trips he was taking were because he had another family."

"Daaaamn. You're making this up."

Tamika lifted her right hand as if she was being sworn into court. "I promise you, I'm not. He had a whole other family."

"Damn," he said again.

"So in a way, it served him right that she was cheating on him."

"At least you got a makeup kit out of it."

They shared a laugh.

Wiping her fingertips on a napkin, Tamika said quietly, "She's pretty. Melissa, I mean. What did you like about her?"

Anton shrugged, not really wanting to talk about Melissa. More than anything, his pride was hurt, thinking about her sending another man sexy pictures and sneaking around behind his back.

"She's responsible and goal-oriented."

"Wow, sounds exciting," Tamika said dryly.

He chuckled. "Okay, Miss Smart Ass, what did you like about your man, Calvin?"

"He made me laugh, and... and he has a big dick and can fuck all night." Anton stared at her, and she shrugged. The shift in the air was noticeable, becoming heavy with tension. "What can I say, his stamina was... wow." She shivered, as if reliving a specific moment.

"Okay, I don't want to hear anything else about your man's dick. Or his stamina," Anton muttered.

"He's not my man anymore."

"Your former man, then," Anton said, annoyed. He ate his last slice of pizza and washed it down with beer.

"Do you think you'll miss her?" Tamika asked.

"You like to talk, huh?"

"What tipped you off?"

Anton laughed and thought about the question for a moment. "Yes, I'll probably miss her, to some degree, but not for long. Our relationship was essentially over. But I think with any breakup, there's always a sense of loss of what you had, and what you could have had."

Tamika nodded. "I get that. My relationship with Calvin wasn't perfect, but we could have been so much more. I had this idealized idea of both of us being successful entrepreneurs and taking our businesses to the next level." She huffed out a disappointed breath. "But after I found out he was cheating, I basically checked out. I guess he checked out, too, because he hasn't tried to touch me in months." She winced, as if saying the words out loud caused her pain.

"Calvin's a damn fool. If you were my woman, I couldn't go a day without touching you," Anton said softly.

Sexual awareness thrummed the air between them.

"You're just saying that," Tamika said, her voice sounding strained.

"No, I'm not."

She swallowed. "We should probably stop now."

She still seemed uncertain, as if she didn't believe him. Yet another reason to kick Calvin's ass, because he made this sexy woman doubt her own appeal.

"We're all done here, so I'll clean up..." she continued. As Tamika closed the empty pizza box, he noticed her fingers were shaking.

She hopped up from the floor, and he followed her into the kitchen with the empty bottles of beer.

"You can put those in the recycling bin, over there," she said, pointing.

Anton dropped them into the container and turned to face her. He didn't say a word. Watching. Waiting.

Smoothing her hands down her hips, Tamika said, "Well, it's late, so..."

Eyes locking with hers, Anton prowled closer. "Don't tell me Tamika's at a loss for words."

"It's rare, but it can happen," she said in a soft voice, gazing up at him.

Anton lifted her chin higher with two fingers, angling her face so they looked directly into each other's eyes. "I meant what

I said. If you were mine, I wouldn't be able to keep my hands off of you. And honestly, I've been thinking about getting you naked all night."

He saw when the air left her lungs, her chest depressing and her breath whispering past her parted lips. As if the words brought her a sense of relief.

Then, in a low voice, she asked, "What are you waiting for?"

❧ 9 ❦

Their mouths locked together, and Tamika clenched her arms around Anton's neck. His lips were soft, yet firm. Sweet and succulent as they moved over hers, the possessive pressure making her head swim as lust flared in her loins like a bonfire doused in gasoline.

Yes. Yes. Yes. She needed this. She needed him. He was a salve for the gaping hole blown in her pride and heart.

Anton's hands climbed up her thighs, bunching her dress as they shifted higher. His tongue slipped between her lips, dipping and swirling inside her mouth as he molded her hips and ass with hands that were almost rough in their urgency. Standing on tiptoe, Tamika pressed her mouth harder to his and rubbed her aching nipples against his hard chest for relief. His expert kisses edged away the hurt and embarrassment of the past week and replaced them with the heat of raging desire.

He pulled the dress straps down her shoulders, lips wreaking havoc on the side of her neck and eliciting helpless whimpers of encouragement. When her breasts were exposed, he gazed at them with darkened eyes.

"Beautiful," he whispered, and reverentially kissed the tops of each, treating them to his wet mouth.

He licked the underside of each breast and sucked the engorged nipples into his mouth. Teasing. Torturing. Forcing Tamika's head to fall back and her body to arch away from the wall. She became lost in the sensations evoked by his mouth, his warm breath skidding over her breasts driving her insane. He seemed to be obsessed with her nipples, grunting his satisfaction as he teased them one at a time in his mouth. His uninterrupted devotion made breathing difficult and forced her to bite her lip to refrain from begging him to stop.

Anton dropped to his knees and used blunt fingers to drag her thong past her knees, right before he pushed up her dress and his tongue darted out to her shaved sex. Tamika cried out and grabbed the top of his head.

She thought she was losing control before, but nothing— nothing prepared her for Anton Bevins' thick lips gripping her engorged clit. She sucked air between her teeth, undulating her hips into the exquisite pleasure of his wicked mouth.

With his hands spreading her ass cheeks, his tongue lashed against her clit. He ate her out like a starving man, as if she was the first and only thing he'd eaten all night. The erotic goodness of his mouth brought her close to fainting, the furious assault on her sex continuing until a rolling orgasm billowed through her body.

She cried out again, louder this time, shaking as pleasure pummeled her body. As the climax wound down, Anton stood and held her head steady with a firm grip. His kissed her hard, pressing his lips to hers in a ravenous demand as his thumbs brushed along her cheeks. His clothes grated against her already sensitive nipples, forcing a moan of frustration from the depths of her chest as she struggled to remain upright on downright shaky legs.

Panting and desperate, Tamika tore at his shirt, popping open buttons and yanking the tail from his waistband. His pants were next, fingers trembling in anticipation as she unzipped him, pushing down his boxers until his dick sprang free like an erotic surprise.

She inhaled sharply, stroking his length in wonder, empowered as he stopped breathing and watched her hand caress from the base to the crown and back again. He was huge. Long, beautiful, dark, and thick. She squeezed him and was rewarded with a low groan, his hips pushing forward until the tip pressed against her belly.

Tamika shuddered at the thought of taking all of him, anywhere he chose—in her mouth, between her legs, in her ass. But Anton was still in control. He lifted her from the floor with ease and pressed against the entrance to her body. In that split second, anticipation swelled in her loins, but Anton came to an abrupt halt. He hesitated. He wasn't wearing a condom and hadn't asked if she had any. She didn't at the moment and didn't care. She wanted him and angled her hips forward to convey the message.

Clutching the back of his head, she whispered, "Please," against his mouth.

The word had barely left her lips before he pushed in and started pumping right away. Tamika joined in the sexual dance, thrusting her hips against his. It was surreal how good he felt. Like heaven and magic all at once.

Anton groaned mightily. "Goddamn. I knew your pussy would feel good, but... *shiiiit*."

She sucked his neck and throat. Whispering words of encouragement in his ear. "More... yes... please don't stop."

"Look at me," Anton commanded.

She did as he demanded, and their gazes tangled together, breaths mingling as their panting betrayed the effort exerted by their connected bodies. She was drawn to this man, linked to him in an inexplicable way. Hypnotized by the power and intensity of his gaze.

Over and over, Anton pistoned between her delicate folds as

he held her gaze, alternating his rhythm between deep and shallow thrusts.

"I'm about to come, baby. Tell me you're close," he panted.

"I'm close. Please, *please*," Tamika begged.

She was on the brink of an orgasm and tightened her throbbing muscles around his length. He temporarily lost his rhythm and swore softly under his breath.

Holding her up with one hand, Anton licked his thumb and pressed it to her clit. With only a few circular rubs, he dragged the orgasm from her loins, and Tamika screamed. She grasped wildly at the empty air with one hand and sank the nails of the other into his shoulder.

"I'm coming," he groaned, sounding like a man in pain. A man at the end of his tether with nothing left to do but give in to the surging storm of sensation.

He pressed her into the wall, both hands gripping her butt cheeks. Pistoning harder and deeper into her body, he buried his face in her neck. He shuddered as both hands tightened on her fleshy cheeks, and he ejaculated with a loud groan.

Neither of them moved for a long time. Clinging to each other, their chests heaved up and down, the sounds of their breathing loud in the quiet kitchen.

Finally, Tamika lowered her bare feet to the floor, and Anton lifted his head. With eyelids that were nothing more than slits, he tasted her lips and she leaned into him, savoring the enticing touch of his mouth against hers.

"Where's the bedroom?" he asked.

Tamika answered by leading the way down the hall and pulling Anton through the door and into the dark room.

He stripped off the rest of her clothes and pushed her onto her back. His limp penis grew hard right before her eyes as his hungry gaze skated over her nude body. Silently, he appraised her full breasts capped by ebony nipples and feasted his eyes on her belly and the decorative white gold ring in her navel. When he moved lower to the flare of her hips and bare pubes—moist from desire and the attack of his mouth—a muscle in his jaw tightened.

"Damn."

Anton came down on top of her and pried her thighs apart. Again he kissed her, resulting in a tangle of tongues and lips that spiked their desire.

"I've been wanting to fuck you since you showed up at my door."

"I've been wanting to fuck you since I showed up at your door," she admitted.

She could hardly think or breathe, choking on desire— opening for him as his hard flesh pressed into her. No foreplay needed. Their bodies were already primed, ready for round two.

Tamika wrapped her arms around Anton's neck, his hard chest pressing into her breasts and his face into the crook of her neck.

"Anton..." she moaned, her voice little more than a whisper.

His thrusts became harder, more aggressive, as if saying his name unleashed a different part of him. She clung to him for dear life, pumping her hips upward to meet each downward stroke.

The slap of flesh and their own panting breaths were all that could be heard in the dark.

Anton covered her mouth with his again, giving her a brutal kiss before placing one leg on the outside of hers and deepening the penetration with a scissors-like position.

Tamika's head fell back and came with a keening cry that filled the bedroom. A sound that was raw, loud, and uninhibited —like a firecracker bursting into flames. She lost all control, her hips pumping quickly, grasping onto each ripple of pleasure that spread throughout her body. She reveled in the ecstasy of the orgasm. Grabbing the mattress. Grabbing him.

Beside her head, the fingers of Anton's left hand gripped the rumpled sheets as he came, and he froze for a second before he shuddered through his climax and collapsed on top of her. Both of them groaning. Both of them depleted. Both of them satisfied —again.

Anton rolled onto his back, shoving air in and out of his lungs.

Tamika was breathing hard, too, as she stared up at the ceiling fan.

"I knew it," she said.

"Knew what?"

She smiled as she turned to look at him. "It's always the quiet ones."

❧ 10 ❧

Tamika slowly awoke and glanced at the man in her bed. Anton was still asleep, turned on his side toward her, softly snoring.

They'd had sex, not once. Not twice. But three times.

She was exhausted. Happy. Happily exhausted.

Smiling to herself and biting her bottom lip, she stared at him. Up close, she saw the lines in his lips, the shadow of a beard starting to appear, and the wispy length of his lashes touching his cheeks. His skin was a little dry, but she could fix him up with one of her homemade masks, if he'd let her.

Probably not. Some men were weird about skincare. Calvin, for sure. She'd tried on several occasions to get him to take better care of his skin, but he'd accused her of trying to turn him into a metrosexual.

Leaning toward Anton, Tamika took a whiff of his skin. Sensitive to smell, she infused many of her products with pleasing aromas, so a good smelling man was a bonus. And Anton smelled *good*. How does someone smell so good first thing in the morning, especially after a night of sex?

The lack of sex with Calvin didn't explain why she was so horny or explain why she wanted to snuggle with an almost stranger. She ached to brush her fingers over his skin but didn't dare because she didn't want to wake him. Instead, she eased from the bed and slipped on her robe, padding into the bathroom so she could be alone with her thoughts.

Last night had been crazy. First the confrontation with Calvin, and then the sex marathon with Anton. She shivered a little as she thought about their night together but wasn't naïve enough to believe their lovemaking was anything more than two broken-hearted people trying to feel better. She was on the rebound and so was he. That was the only explanation for what had happened between them, but she didn't regret it.

⚘⚘

"WHAT ARE YOU LOOKING AT?"

"You," Anton answered.

He sat on the side of the bed with the sheet covering his nakedness from the hips down. Tamika had come out of the bathroom seconds before and stood in the doorway looking sexy as hell in a white silk robe.

"Like what you see?" she asked, lips twisted into a tantalizing smile.

"Definitely."

Anton's gaze moved languidly down her petite and curvaceous body. Her short hair had been brushed neatly back from her face, vastly different from the spiky disarray he'd created by running his fingers through the soft strands last night. The robe clung to her as if it had been painted on, revealing the swell of her soft breasts, the peaks of her nipples, and the roundness of her hips.

Licking his lips, Anton relived her taste, while his olfactory sense reminded him of how she'd smelled—the delicate scent of her skin contrasting with the muskiness at the apex of her thighs.

His adductor muscles tightened a smidge as arousal spiked in his blood. Three times hadn't been enough. He wanted her again.

Before he could express his thoughts and talk her back into bed with him, a phone rang. Anton looked around. "Is that me or you?"

"I think that's you," Tamika replied.

He stood and rummaged through the pile of clothes on the floor until he found his slacks with the phone tucked into the pocket. Instead of answering, he glared at the screen. Melissa was calling, and he didn't want to talk to her. But he had to, because she was probably calling about coming to get her belongings.

"Hello?" Holding the phone between his ear and shoulder, Anton tugged on his boxers. The whole time, he could feel Tamika's eyes on him.

"Good morning," Melissa said. "I, um, I'm calling because I wanted to see if I could come by in thirty minutes to get my clothes and everything."

"That's kind of short notice," he pointed out.

"What's the big deal? I'm only doing this as a courtesy."

"I'm not home right now, so give me more like an hour."

There was silence on the other end. Finally, Melissa asked in a lowered voice, "Did you get up early to go work out?"

He did get up early on Saturday mornings to work out, but he went to the gym at the complex. She knew as well as he did that he wouldn't need an hour to get back to the apartment from that location.

"No." He glanced at Tamika, who did nothing to hide that she was listening to his side of the conversation.

"So you slept out? I mean, it's kind of early for you to be out on a Saturday morning."

"Is that really any of your business right now?" Anton asked irritably.

"You don't have to be rude to me," Melissa said in a wounded voice.

"I'll meet you at the apartment in an hour," Anton said, injecting as much coldness into his voice as he could. "Anything else?"

"Calvin will be with me. Asshole." She hung up without saying goodbye.

"What was that about?" Tamika asked.

"That was Melissa. She wants to come by the apartment to get her things, and she said Calvin was coming with her."

"That's going to be awkward," Tamika said.

"I can handle them. Have you heard anything from him regarding when he'll come by here to pick up the rest of his belongings?"

"Maybe he'll come by after he gets through helping her. Who knows?" Tamika's eyes sparkled with mischief. "I have an idea, leave something behind—like your tie or your jacket."

"What for?"

"So Calvin will know I wasn't alone last night. Even better if he figures out that you're the man who spent the night here."

Her words rubbed him the wrong way.

"Is that why you slept with me?" Anton asked, stomach tightening as he awaited the answer. He knew better. He knew better than to ask a question he might not want to hear the answer to, but he'd asked, anyway.

"What do you mean?"

"Why did you sleep with me?"

"Why did *you* sleep with *me*?" Tamika returned.

"Did you sleep with me to get back at him?"

"Don't tell me there's not a little part of you that feels vindicated after the night we spent together."

He'd be a liar if he denied it, but his emotions were a mess. He was angry at Melissa and disappointed in her behavior. But like Tamika suggested, a small part of him wouldn't mind rubbing it in her face that he'd had mind-blowing sex last night with the woman whose boyfriend she stole. Except he would never articulate that.

"You know what, you talk too much," he said to Tamika.

Anton yanked his shirt off the floor and angrily shoved his arm into one of the sleeves.

"Oh, now you want to pretend like you're Mr. Morality?" Tamika placed her hands on her hips and glowered at him.

"You feel better now that you screwed the ex of the woman who stole your man?"

"Actually, I do. Don't try to pretend you don't feel a sense of satisfaction at getting back at the man who stole your woman. You enjoyed screwing me in Calvin's kitchen and in his bed—and sucking down his favorite beer."

"Like I said, you talk too damn much."

Anton continued getting dressed. Furious, anger burned through him at her accusations. He wasn't sure what was upsetting him more. The fact that she was right, or the fact that he'd expected—no, hoped—there could be more between them. He felt a connection to her, unlike with any other woman before. But she had basically whittled down the night they'd spent together into nothing but revenge sex at their exes.

"And you don't talk enough. You don't want to admit that you're human, like the rest of us."

"Yeah, that's it," Anton said with a bitter laugh.

He sat down on the bed and pulled on his shoes, not bothering to include his socks. Then he stood and shoved his cell phone and socks into his pockets.

"So you're leaving?" Tamika asked as he looked around to make sure he hadn't forgotten anything.

"Yes. What else is there? I got what I wanted. I fucked Calvin's girl. And lucky me, she was a good fuck."

Her eyes widened slightly, and she looked like he'd slapped her. Shame sawed into him as if he'd slapped her. He winced internally and wanted to take the words back, but before he could, Tamika said, "Wish I could say the same about you. Get the hell out of my apartment."

Her words hit hard, robbing him of speech. What the hell did she mean by that?

She left the bedroom in a huff, head held high and back straight as an arrow. Anton followed, flexing his fingers in anger. Seething. He knew she was lying, but she landed an effective blow which struck at his ego, which had already taken a generous beating thanks to Melissa screwing around on him.

He grabbed Tamika around the waist and yanked her back around, instantly going hard as her soft curves pressed up against him.

"What are you doing?" she demanded.

Bringing his face close to hers, Anton murmured, "Are you saying that I didn't satisfy you?"

Her chest heaved up and down. "Barely."

"Four orgasms and a red lipstick ring around my dick says otherwise."

"Women fake orgasms and give pity blow jobs all the time." Eyes shooting sparks, she gave him a tight smile.

Anton ran his tongue along the shell of her ear, and she jerked her head away. "You're a damn liar. Guess I'll have to prove you wrong."

He dragged her by the wrist into the bedroom and tossed her onto the bed. Tamika glared at him, but didn't do anything as he kicked off his shoes and unzipped his pants. He had somewhere to be, but he was burning with desire for this woman. He couldn't think straight for wanting her.

As he came out on top of her, she opened her legs and grabbed his shirt, yanking him closer. Anton forced open her robe and exposed one of her breasts, fastening his mouth over the puckered nipple. His teeth were rough and hard as they grated over the tight bud, and he growled with satisfaction as she released what was clearly an involuntary whimper.

He took his throbbing dick in hand and positioned it at her already dripping entrance.

He was going to make her eat her words.

❧ 11 ❧

Arms crossed and leaning against the counter that separated the small kitchen from the living room, Anton watched the movement in and out of his apartment. At the moment, Calvin was carrying a box of Melissa's belongings out to the pickup truck he had borrowed from a friend. More than once he'd envisioned tripping Calvin on his way out, and after he fell to the floor, jumping on him and punching his face continuously until he was tired.

They were almost finished, so Anton was relieved, ready for this part of his life to come to an end. Anger and disappointment still burned inside him like a hot flame, but he kept his face neutral as he watched the new couple take boxes, luggage, and knickknacks out to the truck.

Of course he'd arrived late because he'd had a point to prove with Tamika. When he showed up at the apartment, Melissa was already there with Calvin, packing up her belongings. She watched him in silence as he entered, her eyes accusatory as they flicked over the same clothes she'd seen him in the night before. If he'd stepped close enough, she would've probably smelled Tamika's scent on him.

Right now, he wore sweat pants and a white tee, and Melissa

was dragging a suitcase behind her as she came out of the spare bedroom, which doubled as his office and a place for storage.

She wore a cropped top and black yoga pants. The top exposed her tight midriff, and the pants showed off her firm thighs and behind. In the past, he would have reached for her when she was dressed like that, and maybe this was her way of making sure that he got a final look at what he was missing, but the truth was he no longer cared. Knowing that she had lied to him for months while she screwed another man was upsetting, to say the least, and the sight of her turned him off.

She stopped in front of him and glanced over her shoulder at the open front door, checking to see Calvin's location.

"We're almost done," she said.

Anton didn't respond.

He hadn't said much the entire time, preferring to supervise to ensure she didn't take anything that belonged to him. He'd been right to do so, stopping Calvin on his way out the door with a lamp Anton had bought years ago.

"You don't have to be so cold, Anton," Melissa said.

"Don't start," he bit out.

"All I'm saying is, we didn't have to end like this."

Unbelievable. Was she actually acting like she had been the one wronged?

He pushed away from the counter but kept a safe distance so he wouldn't be tempted to throttle her. "Our relationship absolutely had to end like this, because you made a decision to be with that guy behind my back. You made a decision to get an apartment with him before you told me you were moving on. So excuse me if I'm not more sympathetic."

"You know why that happened."

"No, actually I don't know why."

"I wasn't happy!" Melissa yelled.

"Then why didn't you leave? Why lie and pretend you were going on a trip?"

Melissa took a deep breath and slowed down. "*Because*, Calvin and I knew after we told you and his girlfriend we were leaving, there'd be a lot of stress and drama. We'd been sneaking around to spend time together—a day here and there. We just wanted a week alone with no pressure."

"Is that supposed to make me feel sorry for you?"

"I would have never cheated if you'd shown you cared, Anton."

"Please, enlighten me. How did I not show that I cared? "

She pointed a finger in his face. "See, that's your problem right there. You're arrogant and you don't like to listen."

"I told you to enlighten me, but I guess Calvin is a better listener?" Anton asked sarcastically.

"As a matter fact, he is. I tried talking to you. Over and over again. But you wouldn't listen."

"Tried talking to me about what?" he asked.

"About me. About you. About us. Why do you live like this, when you can have so much more? You're well off, you make a lot of money, but you live like someone who works the drive through at McDonald's."

He chuckled softly, shaking his head. "So let me get this straight, I should have listened to you and spent more money, is that it? I should have listened to you and moved into a more expensive apartment, which meant that I would be putting away less money for my future. Am I right?"

"*Your* future. Are you listening to yourself? You weren't thinking about me or including me in your plans."

"You wanted me to make plans with you like I was your husband, but we weren't married. No woman is laying claim to my money until we're married."

She glared at him. "It's not only about the money. I don't think you were all in, in our relationship."

"Now that, I have to agree with you. I wasn't all in, because I wasn't sure about you."

"*Me?*" she screeched.

Calvin entered at that moment. "Everything okay in here?"

Anton wanted to tell him to fuck off. Instead, he said, "Everything is fine."

"You can take this out for me," Melissa said, pointing at the large suitcase. Then she pointed to a small box labeled kitchen. "You can take that one out, too."

Calvin watched them both but said nothing, then picked up the box, holding it between his hip and arm, and grabbed the suitcase.

Anton waited until he'd exited before he spoke again. "Let's be real, okay? The truth is, you want someone to boss around. You have that, so there's no need for us to have any more conversations."

"I wanted someone who listened. Who treated my needs like a priority."

"And jumped through the hoops that you set before him," Anton added.

"You never appreciated me, but I'll tell you this, behind every successful man is a good woman. You had a good woman, Anton, and you blew it. Good luck to you."

Melissa stormed into the spare bedroom, and he fought the urge to punch the wall. The nerve of her, to suggest that his success hinged on his relationship with her. She was certainly full of herself.

"Good luck, Calvin," he muttered.

He and Melissa had been together almost two years, but about six months into the relationship, she started hinting around about them not spending enough time together because of his work schedule. He finally gave her a key to his place so she could come and go as she pleased. Then she'd claimed it was more convenient to leave a few items of clothing at his apartment, but those few items turned into a drawer and almost half his closet.

Then she started spending more time at his place than at hers, and he was so busy with work, it was too late before he figured out what she was doing. She gave up her apartment and moved in, saying she didn't see the point of them having two places when she was there most of the time, anyway. The invasion of his apartment had been gradual but effective, and after a while he'd found the intrusion untenable. When he told her a while back that they needed to talk, she effectively kept dodging the conversation. Last week she told him that she was going on a business trip and could talk when she returned. Little did he know she'd planned to ditch their relationship and spring her new man on him.

"Goodbye, Anton," Melissa said, following Calvin to the door.

Anton walked toward them. "Keys," he said, extending his hand.

Melissa swung around to face him. Despite his animosity toward her, he couldn't deny she was an attractive woman. She'd caught his eye at a party, and he'd approached her because she had a beautiful face and nice body. Over time, he made excuses for why her personality didn't quite mesh with his and convinced himself that she had plenty of other good qualities. But the truth was, she wasn't the right person for him. They weren't the right people for each other.

"I left them right there." Melissa jabbed a finger at the apartment and mailbox keys on the coffee table. Then she slammed the door on the way out.

❧ 12 ❧

Because it was a weeknight, the Double Trouble Bar wasn't very busy, but Anton was not enjoying the after-work distraction. He was irritable and jittery, and it was all Tamika's fault. He missed her.

How could he miss someone he barely knew? Someone so different from him. She was talkative and loud. He didn't talk nearly as much and was more reserved. Yet his attraction to her was unmistakable. He thought about her all the time and even asleep he couldn't rest. One time he woke up in the middle of the night after a very vivid dream and reached for her, encountering nothing but empty space and cool sheets. Rest only came after he grabbed the lotion and quickly got rid of his hard-on.

Beside the pool table, Anton watched his two coworkers. He and Marvin were junior attorneys around the same age, while Axel Becker was a senior attorney and about seven years older.

"How long has it been? A month?" Marvin asked, shoving his glasses higher on his nose before bending over the table to line up a shot.

"Something like that," Anton admitted, talking loudly to be heard over the noise in the bar.

A bunch of guys and their girlfriends played at the other

tables—drinking, yelling, and engaging in raucous laughter.

"And you're still thinking about her. Must be love." Marvin took the shot, but the striped ball missed the pocket and bounced off the side.

They'd been talking about dating. Axel was engaged to a woman he'd fallen hard for while on vacation in Belize. Marvin was happily married with a baby on the way. With both men off the dating scene, the conversation had centered on Anton's dating life, or lack thereof.

He admitted that he'd only gone on one official date since his break up with Melissa. He didn't count eating pizza on the floor of Tamika's apartment as a date, but that night had been way more interesting than the one he'd spent two weeks ago with a woman he met online. After a boring conversation over dinner, he'd said good night at her door and gone home to an empty bed. He never called her afterward.

"How well did you know Tamika?" Axel asked. He was dark-skinned with a beard and was Anton's mentor, taking him under his wing and providing guidance on cases.

"I didn't know her well at all. That's the crazy part." So why couldn't he forget her?

"From what you've told us, doesn't sound like you have a lot in common, either."

"We do and we don't." Anton shrugged, thinking about their mutual loss.

"I thought for sure you and Melissa were going to get married," Marvin said.

Anton wrinkled his nose in disgust. "What? This is proof that you're living in some kind of love bubble. You never listen to what other people say. I *told* you I was thinking about breaking up with Melissa."

Axel chuckled and lined up his shot.

Looking unperturbed, Marvin straightened his glasses on his nose. "Not my fault I found the love of my life and can't concentrate on anything else." He grinned.

At first glance, he appeared timid, but Marvin had the confidence of a lion and was as crafty as a fox circling a hen house. While those skill sets served him well as a criminal defense attorney, he also used them to capture the love and attention of his wife—a statuesque former model who topped him by four inches.

"You like rubbing it in, don't you? The fact is, something wasn't right about the way Melissa was acting, and if I wasn't busy working all the time, I probably would have figured out she was cheating."

"At least now you know."

"Yeah, she was boning another man. And ran off with him." The past four weeks hadn't diminished the bitter taste of that pill.

"Didn't you say the other guy—Calvin—stole Tamika's money?" Axel smoothly tapped a solid-colored ball into a side pocket and then started circling the table, looking for another shot.

"Yes, a real jerk."

Axel straightened. "Back to the issue at hand. You can't stop thinking about Tamika, so what do you think that means?"

"Maybe it's a rebound thing," Anton said with a shrug, though he doubted that was the case. "Or some kind of weird attraction because our significant others were cheating on us with each other."

Marvin spoke up. "If that's the case, your mind ain't right, and you need to stay away from Tamika."

"*But*," Anton said, dragging out the word, "she's fine as hell." His thighs tightened at the memory of sliding between her legs and hearing her breathlessly moan, *Please*. He took a swig of beer to cool down.

"From your description of her, she sounds insane. She showed up at your house with a *baseball bat,* man."

Anton laughed at the memory, the first real laugh he'd had in a while. "I know, and she's not my usual type. She's too—"

"Dramatic?"

He tossed the word around in his head for a while. "Maybe that's the word."

"You need to leave her alone and find you a nice, quiet woman who fits your personality. Tamika sounds like bad news."

But nice and quiet sounded so... boring. Tamika was exciting. Sexy. Spicy. Outgoing.

Axel was watching him hard, eyes narrowed. "Did you sleep with her the night you dropped her off at her place?"

Startled, all Anton could say was, "Huh?"

Marvin stepped closer and stared into his face, the pool game completely forgotten as both men focused their attention on Anton.

"We keeping secrets now? Tell me you didn't," Marvin said.

Anton set down his beer and folded his arms across his chest. "Then I'd be lying."

"Now everything makes sense!" Marvin exclaimed. "She's wild, so the sex was probably wild. Don't let it cloud your thinking, man."

"Might be too late," Anton muttered. "I told her she could move in with me." Anton knew the judgment was coming but didn't care.

"You did what?"

"Goddamn," Axel muttered, dropping his stick to the table.

"You heard me."

Marvin stared at him. "Bruh, you barely knew this woman. You already jeopardized your career by grabbing old dude by the jacket. If you'd fought with him, you could have lost your job. The way you're acting, it's not like you. What are you thinking?"

Marvin looked genuinely worried. They were good friends— closer than he was with Axel, and Marvin was used to seeing him behave differently. Calmly. Logically.

"She had nowhere else to go. What was I supposed to do?"

"Most people have somewhere to go. Family or friends.

Sounds to me like she was taking advantage of you because of the situation."

"She wasn't. She turned me down."

"You realize you're doing it again, right?" Axel interjected.

"Doing what?" Anton asked.

"Don't act dumb," Marvin said. "Why you always gotta be the savior, man? Sometimes you have to mind your own business and let things play out."

"The two of you know I can't do that."

Marvin sighed. "Yeah, I know."

One time he analyzed his own behavior after Marvin had accused him of having a savior complex. Self-reflection was not easy, but he did wonder if some of his behavior stemmed from the fact that he hadn't been able to rescue his brother. He may not have been able to save Ricky, but at least he could help other people.

Maybe that was all part of the plan, and he hoped that there was a plan. Because for the longest time, he couldn't reconcile how the universe could've allowed a nine-year-old boy to drown in a river on a sunny summer afternoon.

"I'm not going to judge you," Axel said. "If you're still interested in Tamika, my advice is to go for it but proceed with caution."

Marvin nodded, albeit reluctantly. "He's right. You obviously really care about her if you're still thinking about her after a month has passed. Don't be miserable, I guess."

Anton laughed at the half-hearted advice. "Thanks, I guess."

"I'm going to give you the same advice my father gave me," Axel said. "In case you're still wondering if your interest in Tamika is real or a rebound thing. When it comes to women—the one—you'll know when you find her, because no one else will do."

Marvin nodded his agreement. "Honestly, bruh, it sounds like you found her. I guess you better go get her before someone else snatches her up."

13

"Thank God for the weekend. Those students are going to drive me to drink." Dana flounced into Layla's loft and dropped her bookbag near the door. Though she complained about her job, she loved teaching and enjoyed working with the students, and she often said she couldn't imagine doing anything else.

She was a full-figured woman with glowing brown skin, waist-length dreadlocks, and a ring in her left nostril and one in her septum. Brilliant with an artistic flair, she taught English at Georgia Piedmont Technical college.

Tamika was seated on the sofa next to Layla, who held up a stack of menus. "We can't decide what we want for dinner. Pizza or the Thai place around the corner?"

"Thai place. We haven't eaten there in a while." Dana dropped onto the large armchair across from them and propped her feet on the ottoman.

"Thai it is. The usual?" Layla glanced at them both.

Her complexion was lighter than Tamika and Dana's, and she had a smile that could light up a room. She was a sweetheart but not a push-over, her personality a perfect fit for her work as the personal assistant to a demanding billionaire.

"Yes," Tamika and Dana said at once.

Tamika jumped up from the sofa. "I'll get the drinks. Coke," she said, pointing at Dana, "and water for you?" she finished, looking at Layla.

"You got it," Layla said, picking up her phone to place the order.

Tamika went into the kitchen, passing by a bunch of her boxes stacked against the living room wall. She was still surprised how much stuff she had accumulated during the time she lived with Calvin. Before moving in with him, she had sold or donated a lot of items to accommodate downsizing into a space she shared with someone else. But over time she collected new items —most of them clothes, shoes, and accessories.

Layla insisted that having her there wasn't a problem since she wasn't at home most of the time anyway, spending much of her time at Elijah's. For now, Tamika lived out of boxes, but Layla had brought in a wardrobe where she could put her clothes. She kept the bedroom, and Tamika slept on the sofa.

Her last conversation with her father about her living arrangements hadn't gone well. He wasn't pleased with her decision to stay in Atlanta, but he left the door open in case she changed her mind and wanted to come home to Augusta.

When Tamika returned from the kitchen, Dana asked, "Okay, what did I miss?"

Though Tamika had been staying at the loft for a month, this was the first time the three of them were hanging out together.

They spent the next thirty minutes catching up on each other's lives, pausing when the food arrived, and then diving back into the conversation. They ate in the living room, three different meals spread out on the coffee table family style, passing around paper plates so they could sample each other's food.

Dana had recently ended a relationship, for which she happily exclaimed, "I'm free!" Meanwhile, Layla's relationship with Elijah was going strong.

"You two are so cute," Dana said. She resumed propping her feet on the ottoman as she ate.

Layla nodded, though not as enthusiastically as one would expect considering how much time she spent with her beau. "We're having fun, that's for sure."

"Your turn to spill," Dana said, looking pointedly at Tamika. "Still haven't heard from Anton?" She asked the question hesitantly because she knew he was a sensitive topic.

Tamika shook her head. "At least he followed through on his promise and drafted the contract for Calvin."

She recalled the day the signed contract arrived from Calvin, hand-delivered by courier. When she realized Anton had kept his promise, she'd been extremely grateful and immediately sent him a text of thanks. She'd wanted to call and talk to him but had been too nervous and wasn't sure what to say.

Anton completely threw her off her game. Her emotions were all over the place, up and down like a seesaw, as if she didn't know her own mind. He texted back *You're welcome*, and that had been the last they communicated. But Calvin paid every week, as required by the contract, and that should be enough. It wasn't.

"Well, eventually you'll get your money back, which is a good thing," Layla said.

"Until then, I have to figure out how to get the exposure that I had wanted for my business." She'd planned to have a marketing blitz by running ads and sending out samples to popular bloggers. "I have to recalibrate, and I'm not sure how to. Based on the payment plan, it'll be another twenty-three months before I get all my money back, which pushes me behind schedule."

"If you need a loan..." Layla offered.

"No, you've done enough." Tamika turned to Dana, whose mouth was open and was about to speak. "No, to you, too. I'll figure this out. Push comes to shove, I'll put the expenses on a credit card or ask my dad for a loan."

"I hate you're in this situation, but if you change your mind, my offer still stands," Layla said.

"Same," Dana said.

Grateful, Tamika looked at her best friends. She was lucky to have them. They not only helped her move out of the apartment before the landlord tossed her possessions in the street, they'd helped her get rid of the furniture and other items Calvin had left behind because, according to him, they weren't good enough for his new place. One of Layla's neighbors bought the furniture set in the living room, and Tamika donated the bedroom furniture to an organization where Dana volunteered, helping women transitioning out of abusive relationships.

"Instead of spending a lot of money running ads, is there a way for you to get some free publicity?" Dana asked.

"You mean like doing interviews? I've done that before, but it only does so much," Tamika asked.

Layla snapped her fingers. "My boss has a list of media people that the PR department sends press releases to whenever the company is doing something in the community. Maybe I could hook you up with some of the people on the list? I'd have to talk to the PR department to see if it's a possibility."

"Are you serious? I mean, if you could do that, it would be great. But I'm small potatoes. Would they be interested in someone like me?"

"You have to find the right angle for them to want to do a write up on you. Let me talk to PR and see what they say. They might have some ideas."

"You guys are truly the best. I promise, one day when I'm rich, you're set for life."

Layla laughed and pulled her into a one-armed hug. "I'll be satisfied with free makeup for life."

"Same," Dana said with a grin.

"You have a deal," Tamika said.

"Yay!" Dana said, clapping.

Tamika's phone vibrated on the coffee table, and she picked

it up. When she saw the number on the screen, her heart flew into her throat.

"What's up?" Dana asked, instantly attuned to the change in Tamika.

"It's him," she whispered.

"Answer it!" Layla said.

They both knew she had been longing for more contact from Anton, but after the way they had parted, she didn't have the confidence to reach out to him. Besides, she'd insinuated that their night together hadn't meant much to her—going so far as to suggest sex with him hadn't been great. Boy, did he prove her wrong the next day! She shuddered at the exquisite memories of their out-of-control passion and the way his hard body had angrily thrust into hers—from in front, from behind. How he'd growled, "Look at your ass. You're a damn liar," in her ear as she hollered through multiple orgasms and clawed the sheets.

She'd desperately wanted to reach out to him and admit she was wrong and wanted to see more of him. But what if he didn't feel the same way? She'd be crushed.

But now he was calling, making her heart palpitate at a dangerously fast level.

Taking a fortifying breath, she answered the phone. "Hello?"

"Hi, Tamika. This is Anton."

Hearing his velvety voice after so long was breath-stealing. The insides of her thighs throbbed. Tightening her fingers on the cell phone, Tamika said, "I know who this is."

Ignoring her friends' curious gazes, she kept her eyes on the plate of food, concentrating on the conversation and the emotions swirling behind her ribs.

"I was thinking about you and wondered how you were doing. How have you been?"

"Good." *Better now*, she thought. "I'm settled into Layla's place."

"You have your own room?"

"No, it's a one-bedroom."

"Sounds tight."

"It's okay," she said with a careless shrug. Since her options had been going back home or living on the street, she considered Layla's loft to be a palace.

"Calvin making those weekly payments like he's supposed to?"

Tamika stood and sauntered away from her friends and the weight of their stares. Keeping her back to them, she lowered her voice and replied, "So far so good."

"So you're flush with cash now."

"Hardly," she said with a little laugh, heart aching at his teasing. How could she miss him so much when they barely knew each other? "Thanks again for keeping your word and taking care of that for me."

"Not a problem. Maybe you should take me out as a thank you."

She rested a hand on the back of one of the dining chairs. "I assumed your work was pro bono."

"It was, but..." His voice trailed off, and if she heard him correctly, he muttered something that sounded like *What the hell am I doing?* He breathed deeply and let the air out of his lungs. "Listen, I was wondering if... if you were free. I'd like to take you to dinner—a nice one, with a white tablecloth and good food, and wine."

"Why would you do that?" Tamika asked.

He didn't respond at first, and her stomach tightened with stress as she waited for his answer.

"Because I miss you," he replied. "I can't get you out of my mind. I want to see you. I *need* to see you."

Her heart fluttered crazily in her chest. "I miss you, too. I want to see you, too. When do you want to go to dinner?" She wasn't going to say a word about the half-eaten plate of Thai food on Layla's table.

"Around eight o'clock is good, but I'd like to see you before then. I'd like to see you right now. I'm downstairs."

"What?"

"Come downstairs. Let me see you."

Despite her shock, excitement sizzled in her veins. "I'll be right there." She hung up and swung to face her friends.

"What's going on?" Layla asked.

"He said he misses me, and he's downstairs. He wants me to come down there right now."

Dana's face broke into a wide smile. "Go!"

Tamika took off running and raced down the stairs instead of taking the elevator. When she pushed through the glass doors, Anton was standing on the sidewalk, hands stuffed into a pair of chinos. He wore a faded blue T-shirt with the Superman logo on the front. Like the caped crusader, he was tall, his muscled chest pressing against the soft cotton, the sleeves capped tight around his biceps.

She wanted to rush into his arms, but instead moved slowly in the waning evening light, taking her time so he wouldn't see how excited she was by his presence.

"Hi." She couldn't keep the smile off her face, though.

"Hi," he said.

Tamika stopped a few feet away. "You tracked me down, again."

He laughed, his voice low and sexy. "I did."

"You have some interesting resources. Should I be concerned that you might be a stalker?"

"Absolutely."

He closed the distance between them and looked down at her, his face falling into serious lines. He still hadn't taken his hands out of his pockets.

"I kept thinking you'd probably be out with some guy having a great time tonight."

"I don't go out like I used to. I'm mostly a homebody now. I hit the club scene pretty heavy when I first moved to Atlanta, and I may have danced on a bar top a time or two."

Anton laughed.

"I'm serious," Tamika said.

The smile on his face died. "Oh."

Living under her father's roof as an adult had meant she still had to abide by his rules, and though she went out, she'd been careful about her behavior. When she arrived in Atlanta, she'd partied hard with her co-workers and other friends she'd made, but nowadays, going out to a nice dinner or heading to the bowling alley was all the excitement she could handle.

As they continued to look at each other, the air vibrated with longing and sexual energy.

"I don't know what's happening to me. I don't usually act like this—impulsive," he said. "And I was going to save the next question for later—much later. Maybe another week or so because I don't want to scare you off. But now that I've seen you again, I realize that I have to say what's on my mind. I don't want to see anyone else, Tamika. I don't want date around or slow down so I can figure out if we're right for each other. I already know that we're right for each other, and I want you to move in with me. Now. Today. Can you picture it? You and me together?"

Heart thudding, Tamika gazed up at him. She understood what he meant, about not understanding what was happening. She didn't understand either but was confident she was about to make the right decision and didn't care what anyone thought.

Impulsive was her middle name.

"Yes, I can," she answered.

"So you'll move in with me?"

"Will I have my own bedroom?" Tamika asked.

"Nah. You'll have to share mine."

"Sounds tight."

"But I think you'll like it."

"I'm sure I will." Her smile broadened. "Yes, I'll move in with you."

❧ 14 ❧

Anton exited the car and walked up the steps with his briefcase and the mail he'd picked up from the box. This had been one of the most stressful weeks of his life, but coming home to Tamika made all the difference.

Two weeks in, and he didn't regret his decision to ask her to move in at all. Yes, the question had been impulsive. Yes, he wondered if he was crazy—and so did his friends and family, but he hadn't regretted the decision.

For one, she was usually the first one home, which meant when he arrived, he had the utmost pleasure of being welcomed home by a woman with a big personality. Not to mention she walked around the apartment in short shorts and tight tanks, sweatpants and tight tees, all of which were a feast for the eyes.

Though they shared the bedroom with an ensuite bathroom, he'd given Tamika full reign of the second bathroom in the hall. Lucky for him, he'd done that. When she wasn't at the commercial kitchen, she experimented with and analyzed the product lines of other companies—very evident the one time he went into her bathroom to get a piece of tissue. He'd never seen so much makeup and skincare products outside of a department store.

The moment Anton stepped across the threshold, a delicious aroma greeted him. Another perk of having Tamika live with him was that he sometimes had the pleasure of a home-cooked meal. Last week she'd cooked twice, but this week, she'd cooked every night.

He dropped the envelopes on the glass coffee table and inhaled the enticing scent of simmering spaghetti sauce filled with basil, oregano, and garlic.

The way the apartment was set up, as he entered, he walked into the large living room. Straight ahead was the dining area and the kitchen. On either side of this main space were the bedrooms.

The kitchen wasn't very large, but it was open, with a bar separating it from the living room. There were also large blind-covered windows, a small island in the middle, and black cabinets and stainless-steel appliances for a sleek modern look. To the left, a cubby hole in the kitchen contained a built-in desk that could be used as a bill paying center. Anton had hardly used it, and upon his insistence, Tamika took over that area as a work station, and she stored her boxes and a table for assembling packages in the bedroom he used as an office.

Tamika popped up from behind the bar separating the kitchen from the living room, clutching silverware and napkins in her hands. "Hey! I was getting ready to set the table."

Her energy and bubbly attitude were a welcome change to the gravity of the case he'd worked on all week.

She set down the tableware and walked out wearing a cute little apron tied around her waist. All he saw was her pink cami top, pink bra straps, and bare legs from the knees down. His mind took off in a lusty, dirty direction. Had she been cooking with no pants on?

"Nothing too fancy," she continued, walking toward him. "Spaghetti and meat sauce and salad. Hope you're hungry."

She picked up the mail that he dropped on the table. Now

that she was turned sideways, he saw the gray gym shorts she wore.

"I'm starving," Anton said, looping an arm around her waist and pulling her in for a quick kiss. With her soft body pressed against him, tasting her lips was the best welcome home any man could have. "Mmm."

She grinned up at him and touched his cheek. "Bad day?"

"Kinda. Glad it's over. Glad the week is over and I can relax a little."

"No work for you for the next two days. I'll be watching you."

That was the other thing about Tamika—her laissez-faire attitude about work. No pressure to work harder and spend more money. She wasn't obsessed with appearances the way Melissa had been. Yet despite that lack of pressure, he *wanted* to work harder and spend more money on her.

She headed back to the kitchen, hips swaying, bottom looking full and tight in the thin shorts. She dropped one of the pieces of mail onto the desk.

"You don't have to cook for me every day, you know," Anton said.

"I'm not cooking for you. I'm cooking for us. We can't eat out all the time," Tamika said.

"Well, I appreciate it."

He hated to keep comparing her to Melissa, but this was another way in which they differed. Melissa hadn't been much for cooking. She preferred to order delivery from their favorite restaurants or go out to eat and run up a steep tab from ordering plenty of cocktails and the most expensive dishes on the menu. Most of the time he didn't care because he could afford the bill and wanted to treat his lady well, but this was a nice change.

Tamika tossed a dish towel over her shoulder. "Go change and I'll set the table for us." She turned her attention to the stove and used a wooden spoon to stir the sauce.

Her energy was so different from his. Funny how being with

her brought into stark reality all the areas Melissa had been lacking in—and all the positive aspects of a relationship he'd been missing out on. It was all so clear now because he'd met someone who hit all the right buttons.

Tamika was engaging, funny, and generous. In retrospect, being with Melissa had been a chore, because she insisted he live up to expectations he had no interest in living up to. But Tamika was different. How did Calvin fumble a relationship with such a sexy, fun-loving woman?

Anton shook his head as he headed toward his bedroom. Some men didn't know how good they had it.

He went into the bedroom and changed into jeans and a gray short-sleeved Henley, then returned to the kitchen where Tamika had already fixed his plate, piling it high with spaghetti and meat sauce.

Her parents were both from the island of St. Kitts in the Caribbean, and a few times she prepared Caribbean dishes. Earlier this week they ate curry chicken with rice and plantains. He'd enjoyed the meal so much he'd gone back for seconds. Another night she prepared salt fish and coconut dumplings. Damn, that had been good. He could still taste the gravy, flavorful from the onions and thyme. And who knew coconut went so well with dumplings?

Anton opened the red wine Tamika had picked up on the way home and poured them each a glass. Then they sat down across from each other at the table. Immediately, the rest of the weight from the day lifted off his shoulders as he shared the problems he experienced on a case for one of his clients. When he finished, Tamika updated him on her day. She had left early this morning to work on a new lip balm product and had spent half the day measuring and testing different combinations.

"My labels with the new TamCam logo were sitting outside the kitchen when I arrived, so I spent the latter part of the day putting them on my jars and bottles. Then I put together my shipments and went to the post office to drop off orders that had come in." She smiled across the table at him.

"We both had a productive day," Anton said. Yawning, he stretched his arms above his head. "I'm tired, and ready for bed."

"Go to bed, I'll clean up."

"No way. I'm going to help you put away the dishes, and then *we're* going to bed. I may not get up until noon tomorrow."

She laughed, standing with her plate and glass in hand. "That, I doubt. You'll go to the gym like you did the last couple of weekends. And don't forget you have the birthday party tomorrow afternoon."

"Ah, shit. I forgot about that." Anton followed her into the kitchen with the rest of the dishes stacked in his hands.

Marvin and his wife were having a birthday party for their five-year-old and had invited a bunch of people over.

"Did you get a gift?" Tamika asked.

"Not yet. I'll pick one up on the way there."

He placed the leftovers in the refrigerator and then turned to face Tamika, who was bent over the dishwasher. His loins stirred as he watched her, but he pushed back the instinctive desire to curl his fingers around the back of her neck and bend her over the island. He could easily drag down those little shorts and screw them both into ecstasy.

Tamika placed the last glass inside and then straightened. She glanced around the kitchen, rubbing her hands together as if dusting off crumbs. "That looks like everything."

"Come with me," Anton said.

"To the birthday party?"

"Yes." He walked over and crowded her against the corner. He kissed her cheek and her neck.

"Marvin invited *you*."

"I'm sure he won't mind if I bring a guest. I want you to come. I want you to meet my friends. You don't want to come?"

"Yes, of course, but... I was waiting for you to ask."

He stepped back a little and studied her. "You're an important part of my life now, Tamika. There's never a question of whether or not I want you with me. I *always* want you with me."

"Yeah?" She stepped into him and wrapped her arms around his waist, bringing their bodies flush against each other.

"Yeah." Anton settled his hands on her soft bottom. "I want to get you out of these shorts so bad."

"I can tell." She cupped his hard-on under his jeans.

He reached behind her and turned on the dishwasher and then started walking backward and pulling her with him, arms securely around her body. "You're gonna let me?"

"I have emails to check and bookkeeping to do."

"Do them later, after I'm done."

"After you're done doing what?"

Anton easily lifted her and she flung her arms and thighs around his body.

"After I'm done making you scream my name."

"I thought you were tired."

"I'm never too tired to make love to you." Then he captured her mouth and kicked the bedroom door shut.

❧ 15 ❧

The birthday party was in full swing by the time Anton and Tamika walked around the side of the house to Marvin's backyard.

Kids were playing in the bouncy house while being supervised by one of the parents in attendance, and a clown and his assistant painted faces and made balloon animals.

"Hey! You made it!"

A slender woman with a protruding belly and a toddler on her hip approached them.

"Hey, Erica, how are you doing?" Anton said.

"Tired," she laughed.

She was a beautiful woman, and Tamika could see why she had been a former model. She was tall, with great bone structure, but more than that, she exuded charm and a positive energy.

"This is Tamika," Anton said, resting a hand at the small of her back.

"Hi, Tamika, I'm Erica, the birthday boy's mommy."

"Nice to meet you. You have a lot of people here."

"I know. This was all Marvin's idea, so I'm a bit overwhelmed, but he loves to spoil the kids." She shot a fond glance over toward the large grill. Marvin was cooking while two other men stood nearby drinking sodas.

"Why don't you go join them?" Erica said to Anton. "I'll take that." She extended a hand for the gift bag in his.

"No, I'll take that. You already have your hands full," Tamika said with a laugh.

"You sure?" Anton frowned at Tamika.

She appreciated his concern but was perfectly fine mixing and mingling on her own.

"Yes, go join them. Do you need help with anything?" she asked Erica.

"Actually, I could use a hand taking the food from the kitchen. We had some of the meal catered, but I didn't want to put out the dishes until Marvin was almost finished on the grill, and he told me a few minutes ago that he'll be done in ten minutes."

"I can absolutely help with that."

"Holler if you need me." Anton kissed her cheek.

Erica rolled her eyes. "She'll be fine, Anton. We won't abuse her, I promise."

Anton chuckled. "Why you always gotta harass me, Erica?"

"Bye." Erica put her arm around Tamika's shoulder and guided her toward the house.

Tamika waved at Anton over her shoulder.

"He's so protective, I swear," Erica muttered. "But it's a nice quality to have. He's a good guy."

"Yes, he is."

When they entered the house, another woman was in the kitchen.

"Tamika, this is Naphressa. She's Axel's fiancée. He's the guy in the green shirt at the grill. He works with Anton and Marvin. Naphressa, this is Tamika, Anton's girlfriend."

"Nice to meet you."

Naphressa had dusky-dark skin and raven hair that spiraled

to her shoulders in wide, lustrous curls. She extended her hand and Tamika shook it.

"So you're the one Axel said has Anton acting all out of character," Naphressa said.

"Yep, she's the one," Erica said with a grin.

"Wait a minute, the two of you have been talking about me and Anton?"

"Oh yes. Tell us your secrets," Erica said.

"Sweetie, I don't think you need any more help. You have two babies and one on the way. You're good."

The three of them fell out laughing, and from that moment on, Tamika had made new friends. She, Erica, and Naphressa took their time transporting the food from the kitchen and placing the dishes on a long table. While they worked, one of the other mothers jumped in to assist.

On the third trip out, Tamika paused to watch Anton chase some of the kids around the yard. The five-year-olds were laughing and squealing, having the time of their lives. But what struck her as interesting was that Anton was having a great time, too.

Warm fuzzies entered her chest. Watching him with those children was... heartwarming. Yet another reason to convince her that while the decision to be with him had been impulsive, she'd acted wisely. She never thought much about having kids, but seeing Anton playing with the boys and girls in the back yard created a fantasy in her head. One where she considered that one day, he'd be playing with their kids the same way.

❦

"No, no, and no."

Anton tried to push past Tamika out of the bathroom, but she stepped in his path and blocked his exit. They both knew he could lift her out of the way, but he stopped, staring up at the ceiling in mild annoyance.

After night fell at the birthday party, parents returned to pick up their kids, and the ones who'd stuck around fixed plates of food and cake to take with them. Tamika and Anton stayed behind with Erica and Marvin, helping them clean up before they said goodbye.

Considering they'd been at a kid's party, Tamika had a lot of fun, chatting with the adults, playing cards, and then jumping around the bouncy house with the birthday boy and his friends.

"Try it. One time. That's all I ask," she said, holding up the jar of product she'd mixed last night, a moisturizing mask she used on her own face. She'd made extra because she wanted to use the mixture on him. "Your face is a little dry, Anton."

Moments before, he'd finished up with his shower, a towel wrapped around his waist, when she accosted him with her idea.

"So you butter me up with dinner all week and then you spring this on me."

"That is not true!"

She liked making him dinner, especially knowing that he didn't have that before, and he made such a big deal about each meal, she found herself scouring the internet for recipes to try. Besides, she had to eat, too, so cooking for them was one way to ensure they both ate, and ate well. One thing she did appreciate was his adventurous spirit. Calvin used to turn up his nose at the Caribbean dishes she made, but Anton dived in and praised each and every meal she created, as if she were the chef in a fine dining restaurant. His enthusiastic responses made her want to continue feeding him when he came home from work.

"My face is fine. I'm not ashy."

"You don't have to be ashy to be dry. My trained eye can see the dryness when we're up close."

"I'll put more lotion on my face."

He picked up the bottle from the counter and Tamika snatched it from his hand and slammed it down.

"Seriously? You really think it's appropriate for you to keep using lotion on your face when your girlfriend is a freaking cosmetics expert?"

"It's lotion for my body. My face is part of my body."

Tamika glared at him.

Anton sighed.

They'd been arguing for the past two minutes, ever since she suggested that he allow her to put on the mask.

"I'm not walking around with a mask on my face," he said.

"This is the twenty-first century, darling. It's okay to take care of your skin. No one will think you're less of a man because you do."

He didn't say a word, and she accepted they were at a stand-off, but she would not lose. She'd hold out until she broke him.

Finally, Anton asked, "What's in it?"

He was asking questions now. Progress!

She held it up to his face. "All products that are good for your skin. Avocado, yogurt, Vitamin E, and a pinch of turmeric. Before I put it on, we'll wash your face with a gentle cleanser to get rid of any excess dirt, and then apply the mask."

"How long do I have to leave this goop on my face?" He removed the jar from her hand and sniffed the contents.

"It's not goop," Tamika said, slightly offended. "It's a moisturizing mask. Fifteen minutes. I'll set a timer."

"All right, I'll try it," Anton said reluctantly, looking less than enthusiastic.

"Yay!" Tamika bounced on her feet. She handed him the cleanser and watched him wash and dry his face. When he finished, she said, "Sit."

Anton settled on the lid of the commode while Tamika used a wood craft stick to give the mixture another quick stir to evenly distribute the ingredients.

"You're way too excited about this. You're using me as a guinea pig," Anton muttered, eyeing her warily.

"Shush, I'm not using you as a guinea pig. I've been putting this mixture on my face for months, so if anyone is the guinea pig, I am."

She moved to stand in front of him, and Anton rested his hands on her hips.

"Anton..." she warned.

"What? If I'm going to let you do this, I should get something out of it." He smiled sexily at her and ran his hands high up on her waist, right below her breasts.

Her skin tingled at his touch, but she refused to be diverted from her task. "Close your eyes so I can apply this 'goop' on your face, please."

He shut his eyes, and she scooped out the product with her fingers and smoothed it onto his skin, careful not to get too close to his eyes.

Once finished, she said, "Open."

Anton stood and examined his face in the mirror while she rinsed her hands.

"How does it feel?" she asked.

"Feels okay," he replied.

Tamika set the timer on her phone for fifteen minutes, and they left the bathroom. In the bedroom, Anton lay flat on his back and stared up at the ceiling.

Tamika straddled his thighs. "Fifteen minutes will pass before you know it, and then you'll be so happy that you did what I said."

He looked at her through slitted eyes. "We'll see."

"While we're waiting, I have some news. I checked my email while you were in the bathroom, and I got an interview with a reporter about my product line!" She released a happy squeal.

Anton raised up on his elbows. "Which newspaper?"

His eyes brightened with excitement for her, making Tamika appreciative that she could share this moment with him.

"The *Fulton County Chronicle*, one of the oldest, most respected papers in the state, in their community profile section. Layla hooked me up with the reporter, who was looking for a small business to mention in that section. I've been interviewed about my products before, but this is the first time I'll have a newspaper interview. The other times have been beauty blogs, and I got a little cross promotion from a couple of makeup artists who viewed my products on Instagram."

"You're about to enter the big leagues," Anton predicted.

"No, I'm not." She dismissed his prediction but excitement rose inside her. One day she hoped to have a feature in a major magazine.

Anton sat up all the way and hugged her waist. "You are. This is only the beginning."

Tamika rested her hands on his shoulders. "We'll see, but I can't deny that I'm excited. She's going to take pictures of my workspace and talk about my background and the products I've launched over the years."

"Free publicity means more sales," Anton said.

"Yep, and I'm ready for the dollars to start rolling in."

Before long, the alarm went off, signaling the end of the fifteen-minute wait. They returned to the bathroom, and after Anton washed off the mask, Tamika patted his face dry with a towel.

"How does your skin feel?" she asked.

"Feels okay." He moved closer to the mirror and examined his face. "Looks good, too, I guess."

"You'll see significant results after a few more applications. Trust me, your skin will thank you for using this product. Your friends will notice the difference, and they'll be begging you for your secret."

Anton laughed. "I doubt that. My friends don't notice much." He rubbed a hand across his jawline. "How often am I supposed to use this?"

"Once a week is enough. Don't worry, I'll remind you."

"And here I was, thinking I was one and done." He looked down at her from lowered lids.

"Oh no, I take care of my man. Once a week, we're doing our faces."

"Can't wait," Anton said, with a tight, fake smile.

"Whatever. Mark my words, you'll be on your knees showing your appreciation soon enough."

Tamika raised up on her tiptoes and gave him a quick kiss before she sashayed away.

❧ 16 ❧

A nton poured himself a glass of orange juice as Tamika lifted a piece of bacon into her mouth.

"If you have time today, meet me downtown and we can get together for lunch," he said, lifting the glass to his lips.

"I probably won't have time. Between talking to the temp agency and trying to catch up on all those orders, I'll have a full day."

The feature in the paper had been published, and sure enough, she'd seen an uptick in orders ever since. They didn't know how long the spike would last, and though Tamika never complained, he could tell she was a little stressed. He was glad she'd finally taken his advice and started the process of getting additional help by talking to a temp agency. She needed to be in a position to handle the increase in manufacturing once she did a big marketing push, and no better time than now to get people trained and ready to go.

Anton drained his glass. "In that case, I'll see you when I get back."

"Have a good day."

Tamika sat down in front of the computer, and Anton patted his pockets, checking for his keys and wallet before he left. Once he was certain he had everything, he leaned down and kissed her cheek. "Later."

He was walking away when he heard her gasp. He turned around to see Tamika staring at the computer screen, one hand over her mouth.

"What's wrong?" He moved swiftly to reach her side.

She looked at him with wide-open eyes. "I don't know what happened overnight, but I have thousands of new orders. Way more than when I closed up shop yesterday."

"*Thousands?*"

Anton stepped behind her and looked at the screen, and sure enough, there were thousands of new orders. His mouth fell open. "Holy shit. What happened?"

"I have no idea. What am I going to do? I don't have any temps yet, and I didn't anticipate such a huge spike. What the hell happened?" With every sentence, her voice raised an octave.

"Okay, calm down. Let's think about this for a minute."

"I can't remain calm!" Tamika screeched. "I can't fill all these new orders. Anton, what am I going to do?"

She jumped up from the chair and started pacing the living room.

"You're going to fill those orders," he said with confidence.

"How? I was already behind on the ones that came in this week. I thought for sure I'd have time to get the temps so I could catch up."

"And you're going to catch up."

"*How?* There's no one else but me." He saw nothing but raw panic on her face.

"I'm going to help you," Anton said.

Tamika shook her head vehemently. "You have to go to work." Tears filled her eyes.

"No, I don't. I'm going to call in sick and come to work with you."

"You have a very important job. You can't do that."

"Actually, I can. I have plenty of leave, and I never call in sick.

We're going to spend the next couple of days catching up these orders. While I call the office, you call the staffing company. We're going to need more than one temp, apparently. Figure out how many people you need based on the number of orders, let them know, and tell them you need help right away."

Whatever had occurred to cause the spike in sales, those numbers probably wouldn't die down any time soon. Tamika nodded but remained frozen, so Anton walked over and gripped her shoulders.

"Tamika, you got this."

"I got this," she repeated, with much less confidence than he did.

She picked up the phone from the desk.

While she made her call, he made his. Because he didn't take much leave and had never called in sick before, human resources was concerned but didn't give him a hard time. He hung up and hurried over to where Tamika sat on the chair in front of her desk. He listened to her side of the conversation, learning that they couldn't get anyone out there until Monday, but they could send over the three temps she requested. That meant she had to handle all of those in-coming orders between now and then, which was four days away. And from the looks of her screen, the orders weren't slowing down.

When she hung up, Tamika buried her head in her hands.

Anton lowered to his haunches and pulled her hands away from her face. "Here's what we're going to do. I've seen this a million times with the companies I work for, okay? Expansion is hard, but not impossible. All we have to do is fill these orders and get you through the weekend until your temps can get here and you can get them trained. I can help you, but is there anyone else you can think of who'd be willing to help?"

She snapped out of her fear and answered, "Dana and Layla. They'll help. Maybe not tonight, but definitely on the weekend."

"Okay, give them a call. In the meantime, I'm gonna go change. We're going to get through this, okay?"

She gazed up at him in awe. "You said 'we.'"

"Of course." Anton smiled. "Let's go. We got orders to fill."

He gave her a quick kiss and then hurried into the bedroom to change.

⚜

TAMIKA DIDN'T KNOW WHEN SHE HAD EVER WORKED SO HARD, but at least she wasn't alone. Anton was there, her friends Layla and Dana had been at the kitchen since Saturday morning, and Marvin had shown up last night and was still there twenty-four hours later.

The five of them had spent the weekend filling orders that came through and had developed a smoothly running system. Layla helped Tamika create product from her instructions, and she also unpacked ingredients and supplies that came in, which Tamika had placed a rush order on. Dana helped create products and put labels on jars, while the men put together orders, affixed the shipping labels, stacked the boxes, and then loaded them in the car for delivery. Over the weekend, the group had made multiple trips to the post office, and all the packages they put together tonight were being stacked by the door. At the end of the night, they'd get taken out to their cars for delivery on Monday.

Tamika kept everyone hydrated and energized with water, Gatorade, and food trays delivered from a nearby deli. She also cranked up the music to keep them in a good mood. But they were doing hard work, and she insisted that her friends take breaks. At the moment, Marvin was in the car, the front seat reclined, taking a nap until he came back in for another shift.

Yesterday she discovered the reason for the spike in sales. The Associated Press picked up the story about TamCam Cosmetics in the *Fulton County Chronicle*, and the article went out to newspapers and websites around the country. The flow of orders continued, with thousands more that needed to be filled, but at least she had been able to put a dent in the ones that came in over the weekend.

"We're almost done," Dana said, setting aside what looked to be the last tube of lip balm to cool on the counter.

Tamika rested her hands on her hips and surveyed the kitchen. She'd spent a small fortune having supplies delivered Next Day Air to meet demand. But, since her friends were working for free, she made good money getting her products out the door.

"I'm all done over here," Layla announced. She wiped sweat from her brow with the back of her hand.

"What else do you need us to do?" Dana asked.

"I think that's it. I'll have more supplies tomorrow and the temps will be here. If you could put more labels on the jars, that would be great."

Dana saluted and went to work.

Tamika went over to where Anton was working at the shrink wrap machine. "How's it going?"

"Doing fine. You okay?" His concerned gaze swept her face.

"I've been better," she admitted. A wave of nausea hit her a few minutes ago, but she hadn't wanted to stop. "Tired," she said.

"You need to take a break."

"I can't. There's too much to do."

"And it will get done, but not if you're—"

His voice broke off as a dizzy spell made her sway in front of him. He caught her and lifted her in his arms.

"That's it. Time for you to get some rest."

"I'm fine," Tamika protested, though she clung appreciatively to him.

Anton ignored her and marched toward the door.

"Is she okay?" Layla asked, sounding alarmed.

"I'm taking her outside to get some fresh air."

Outside the building, he placed her on her feet and forced her to sit on the steps.

"What do you need?" Anton asked.

Tamika felt as if she were going to throw up. "I don't know where this is coming from. I'm queasy and tired, as if I'm sick."

"You're exhausted," Anton said in a hard voice.

She nodded, rubbing her stomach. "Could you get me some water, please?"

"I'll be right back."

He left her alone, and as Tamika's stomach churned, she wished she could feel better. She had so much work to do, she absolutely couldn't fall sick. Then, unexpectedly, her stomach lurched, and she threw up on the side of the steps.

Crap. What the heck was wrong with her? She wasn't the only one working hard here, so why was she so affected?

Anton rushed to her side and handed her a bottle of water. "Sweetheart, you gotta take better care of yourself. I understand this is a big opportunity for you—"

"Anton, I can't slow down now. This is my dream. This is bigger than my dream. Free publicity and everything is going great. I'll take a nap, like Marvin is doing, and then I should be fine."

His jaw line firmed. "I don't like this."

"I'm not working harder than anyone else."

"Actually, you are," he said, his voice taking on a scolding tone. "You been going practically nonstop, and I warned you about that. What are you going to do tomorrow, when you have to continue working and your friends aren't here?"

"Push through."

"I know this is your dream—"

"I'm not stopping now," she said angrily, cutting him off. She rinsed out her mouth and then took a swig of water.

Looking exasperated, Anton ran a hand over his head. "I can stay with you again tomorrow."

She shook her head vehemently. "You've done enough. You need to get back to work." He'd done plenty, working with her since Thursday and recruiting his friend, Marvin, to help.

"As far as the firm knows, I'm sick, and I still have plenty of time I can take. I can't stay away for too long because of my cases, but I can definitely help you tomorrow. Okay?"

She nodded, relief washing over her that he was willing to set aside his work yet again to help her. But she hated to see the worry in his eyes.

Anton took a seat beside her and squeezed her into his chest. Kissing her temple, he said, "You're not in this alone."

"I know. Thank you," Tamika said quietly.

A few minutes later, she was back inside, working side-by-side with Anton and her friends. Marvin came in later and jumped right back in to help Anton with the packing and stacking.

At the end of the evening, they loaded up the cars, each person promising to deliver their packages to the post office the next day. Tamika was teary-eyed and happy that she had such good friends and such a good boyfriend. On the way home, she fell asleep in the passenger seat, and Anton helped her into their apartment. He undressed her and helped her get under the covers before joining her.

Exhausted, Tamika fell fast asleep, worried that her symptoms weren't simply from being tired.

❧ 17 ☙

Tamika fumbled to answer the phone as she entered the apartment.

"Hello?" she said.

"Where are you?" Dana asked.

"I just came back into the apartment." She locked the door and headed toward the bedroom she shared with Anton, a drugstore plastic bag in one hand.

"Do you have it?" Dana asked.

"Yes. I bought two."

She dumped the pregnancy tests on the bathroom counter and stared at them. She'd been tired a lot lately, and the dizzy spell and episode of throwing up over the weekend reminded her that she hadn't had a period in a while. At first she'd simply forgotten, and then she'd convinced herself that her work schedule was why her period hadn't started yet. But after Sunday, she could no longer avoid the probability of what might be happening inside her body. She could no longer pretend away the truth. She had to face the situation head on.

"Are you okay? Do you need me to be there?" Dana asked.

Dana taught a morning class, and Tamika couldn't allow her

to come over simply to hold her hand while they waited for the results.

"Thanks, but I'll be fine. I'll take the tests and call you after I get the results."

"Okay, talk to you soon."

Tamika hung up the phone and stared at her reflection in the mirror. She saw the worry in her own eyes. She hadn't considered being a mother so soon but was fairly certain she could handle this particular twist in life. The issue would be Anton's reaction. They'd only been together for a couple of months, and though she had no doubt he would make a great dad *someday*, she was fairly certain he didn't want to be a dad *right now*.

She'd read somewhere that the first pee of the morning was best, so she'd hidden the tests in her car last night and came back into the house after Anton left for work. Now she really had to go.

She tore open the first box and peed on the stick and then set it on the counter on a piece of toilet tissue. She set the alarm on her phone and then went into the kitchen to get some water. Her hands were shaking as she lifted the glass to her mouth.

A mother. She could possibly become someone's mother in six months or so. Biting her bottom lip, she fought the smile that threatened to overtake her face. There was so much she wanted to do—career wise—but was it crazy that she didn't mind becoming a mom? Especially with a man like Anton as the father.

The alarm went off, and she drained the water from the glass and went back into the bathroom. She moved carefully over to the counter, as if walking on hot coals, and stopped the timer. Then she dragged her gaze to the test.

Positive.

Emotions warred in her chest. Elation. Anxiety. Fear.

"One more," she told herself.

She busied herself with bookkeeping and other tasks she

could complete on the computer, as well as checking in with the temps. An hour later she took the second test. Same result.

Positive.

Tamika sat on the commode lid, staring at the two pregnancy tests in her hands. She was still shaking, and the tightness in her stomach had only worsened. Part of her had hoped the first result was a false alarm, but the lines on the second test proved there was no mistake.

She was pregnant.

She closed her eyes and took a deep breath, releasing the air from her lungs very slowly. She had to tell Anton. He was definitely the father because she and Calvin had stopped having sex before they split. Anton was the only man she'd been with since then. Anton was the only man she'd been careless with.

She sent short texts to Dana and Layla with promises to talk to them later, and then she went back to work.

❦

"HEY, TAMIKA, I'M HOME!" ANTON CALLED AS HE WALKED down the hall. In the bedroom, he rapped twice on the bathroom door. "You here?"

She'd worked late the past few nights, so he didn't know if she was home or not.

"One minute," she called out.

He frowned because her voice sounded strange. Overly bright. Overly excited. He walked into the closet and removed his shoes and tossed his shirt in the hamper. He was in the process of removing his undershirt when Tamika exited the bathroom.

"Hey," she said.

He tossed the shirt on the pile in the hamper, gaze scouring her face. "You okay?"

Nodding, she nervously rubbed her hands together. "Sort of."

"Sort of? Is there something wrong with your business?"

She'd been working with the temps a few days now. He'd thought for sure everything had been going well.

"No problem with the business, but we need to talk."

Uh oh.

Apprehension balled up in chest. "Whenever a woman says we need to talk, that's never a good thing."

He softened the words with a smile, but when she didn't return the smile, the corners of his mouth fell into a straight line. Now he was really worried. "What's going on? You look like you're about to cry."

"What I have to tell you is really serious," Tamika said, rubbing her palms together.

"Okay," Anton said slowly. He took a seat on the edge of the bed and held his breath.

"I care about you a lot. And whatever you have to say, when I tell you what I have to say, I completely understand. Because this is a lot. I know."

"Spit it out, Tamika. You got me worried."

"I-I'm pregnant." She whispered the words, staring at the carpet, standing before him with her hands clasped together.

"Pregnant?" Stunned, all Anton could do was stare.

She lifted her gaze. "Like I said, I don't expect anything from you. I mean, obviously I would expect you to be a responsible adult because it takes two to tango, but —"

"Wait a minute, wait a minute, slow down." Anton stood. "You have to know by now that I'm not the kind of man to walk away from my responsibility."

Tamika nodded.

"Do you want to keep it?" he asked.

"Yes."

He swallowed, the rate of his heart accelerating. What was she thinking? How was she feeling? He couldn't be sure because she didn't give much away, though she didn't exactly look happy. At least she wanted to keep their baby.

"We're in this together, Tamika."

"Sure."

She rushed out of the room.

"Where you going?" Anton followed her through the door.

"I'm going to Layla's. I wanted you to know, and I can be out of here—"

Anton's heart jolted in panic. "Out of here? What are you talking about?" He grabbed her arm and forced her to turn around and face him. What the hell was going on in her head?

"You didn't sign up for this, did you? You helped me out by giving me a place to stay, and now look at this mess."

If he didn't know better, he'd think she was trying to convince him to break up with her because of the baby—to lay the blame at her feet, as if he hadn't been a willing participant.

"First of all, I didn't ask you to move in simply to give you a place to stay. I wanted you here, as part of my life. You already know that. Second, you didn't get pregnant by yourself. I kinda had something to do with it because, as you pointed out, it takes two to tango. We were both careless, and we both knew what the consequences could be. I don't want you to leave tonight or any other time."

She let out what could only be described as a relieved breath. "What are we doing, Anton? I'm pregnant. It's not like we planned it. This was a mistake. "

"A mistake for who? You said you want to keep the baby."

"I do, but—"

"Yes, we haven't been together very long, and we moved in together right away. We haven't exactly been moving slow, but I've never felt about anyone the way I feel about you."

A tentative smile crossed her lips. "At first, your reaction..."

He rubbed his hand up and down her arm. "I didn't plan on becoming a father anytime soon, and I had to process what you said. We need to spend time together, discussing this before we bring other people into the conversation, and that includes your girls."

He took her hand and led her to the sofa where they sat

down. Anton remained silent for a few seconds before he spoke, looking deeply into her eyes. "I love you, Tamika. I've been wrestling with that for the longest, trying to figure out how to tell you. But I do. And yes, your pregnancy has taken me by surprise, but I'm not... sorry. Actually, I'm more worried about you because you have a future that you're planning. You want to grow your business."

"I'll figure out the growing my business part, but... did I hear you correctly? Did you say you love me?" She whispered the question.

"Yeah. For some reason. I don't know why."

She giggled and climbing onto his lap, looped her arms around his neck. "I know why."

"Why?"

"Because I'm irresistible."

"True."

"And sexy."

"Indeed."

"And funny and fun. And there's no one else like me on the planet."

"All true. And you're mine."

Anton kissed her luscious full lips, smoothing his hands up and down the curve in her back.

Tamika cupped his face, rubbing her thumb across the tuft of hair on his chin. "I love you, too, Anton. I'm certain we were meant to be together."

"No doubt," he said. And kissed her again.

❧ 18 ❧

Tamika woke up when Anton eased away from her. She'd fallen asleep on his shoulder, and being the clingy sleeper that she was, remained pushed up against him, one leg between both of his and an arm thrown across his chest.

"Noooo," she moaned sleepily. "Don't leave." She tightened her arm around his waist and held him hostage.

He laughed and pretended to struggle. "Gotta go to work. And you're keeping me back."

Anton slapped her arm, and she groaned as he slipped from under the covers.

"What's on your agenda today?" he asked with a full body stretch.

They'd both slept naked last night. His muscular arms reach toward the ceiling, and his torso and thigh muscles tightened in the stretch.

Tamika pulled the top sheet up over her bare breasts and watched him walk around the bed toward the bathroom. His nude body was a delight to behold. Tight muscles everywhere, covered in beautiful brown skin.

"I'm going to talk to the temp agency about hiring another temp."

"Orders still coming in faster than you can fill them?" Anton paused at the bathroom door.

"Yes, which is a good position to be in."

"That's right. You can't be afraid of success."

"Don't be afraid of success," she repeated with a yawn, as he disappeared into the adjoining bath.

Tamika waited a few minutes before dragging out of bed and went to the drawer that held Anton's T-shirts and stumbled upon a three-pack of baby onesies.

Busted.

She held up the package and smiled. He'd fussed at her for spending money on baby items too soon, and now she'd discovered he had sneaked and bought some, too. According to the image on the label, one was gray and white striped, the white one had a purple elephant on the front, and the third was designed with yellow giraffes all over the entire outfit. She rummaged through the drawer but didn't find anything else for a baby. Of course not. She was actually the weak one, pouring over online catalogs and constantly adding items to her wish list. She really, really wanted a girl and hoped she and her daughter could have the same close relationship she and her mother did before she passed. She already knew the name she'd give her. Camela.

Tamika blinked back tears mixed with pain and joy and slipped the package back in place underneath Anton's clothes. She pulled on one of his white T-shirts and entered the bathroom. He was still in the shower, and she listened to the water run as she examined her hair. Once she'd snuggled up with him last night, she'd been too lazy to get out of bed to get her satin cap, and her hair had paid the price for her decision. Tunneling her fingers through her dry, messy hair, she wrinkled her nose in disgust. She might wear a hat today instead of making the effort to fix it.

She grabbed her toothbrush and started brushing her teeth. A moment later, Anton stepped out of the shower.

"I see you bought some onesies," she said, arching a brow.

Anton paused in rubbing his skin dry. "You went through my shit?"

Tamika laughed. "I wasn't going through your shit—well, not on purpose. I was looking for a shirt to wear, and I saw the onesies tucked under your shirts."

"I need to find a new hiding place," Anton muttered, wrapping the towel around his waist.

"No, you need to stop buying baby clothes, like you told me to do. We don't know if we're having a boy or girl yet."

"That's why I bought unisex onesies." He tapped the side of his head with his forefinger, and Tamika rolled her eyes. "And you're one to talk."

"What do you mean?" she asked innocently.

He came up behind her and lanced a reproving look at her in the mirror. "You think you're slick hiding your packages, but I saw the bag on top of the shelf in the closet. Did you forget I'm tall? The bag was sticking out behind your hat box."

"I don't know what you're talking about," Tamika said around her toothbrush. She scrubbed her teeth harder.

"You don't know anything about a six-pack of booties, a yellow T-shirt for a *three-year-old* that says, 'My Mommy is the Best,' baby sandals, or—"

"Carter's was having a sale! Get off my back, okay?"

Anton laughed. "I knew you weren't going to stop."

"Whatever. You're as bad as I am."

Anton slipped an arm around her waist and cradled her belly with his palm. "Do you feel anything yet?" he asked.

She finished up and ran the brush under water. "Not yet. From everything I've read, it's unlikely I'll feel the baby flutter anytime soon." At her doctor visit last Friday, she learned she was nine weeks pregnant.

"When do you want to tell your dad?" He kissed her shoulder through the shirt.

"Soon, maybe later this week." Her father wouldn't be pleased, and she wasn't ready for his judgment yet. She wanted a little more time to enjoy this happy period with Anton.

As she rinsed with mouthwash, he remained behind her, watching.

Finally, her eyes met his lighter ones in the mirror. "You look deep in thought. What are you thinking about?"

He closed both arms around her and brought his face beside hers, so they were cheek to cheek. She leaned back into him.

"Marry me," he said, never taking his eyes from her.

Tamika drew a sharp breath and blinked. Then she laughed uneasily. What was he doing? What was he saying? "Because of this?" She placed her hands on top of his on her belly.

"No. Because I'm crazy about you. Because I love you. Because I want to build a life with you."

Her heart stilled as pressure built in her chest. "You don't have to do this, Anton."

"I do. I need to. I need you. Marry me." His eyes were intent and serious, his voice solemn.

Tamika became teary-eyed. "Okay."

"Okay?" He lifted an eyebrow and his head.

"Yes."

"I was hoping for a more enthusiastic response."

She turned to face him and flung her arms around his neck. "Yes! Yes!"

He grinned. "That's more like it."

Tamika laughed and lifted onto her toes, but she quickly sobered, looking him squarely in the eyes. "If you're sure. There's no rush, and I don't want you asking me to marry you because you think I need to be married. We can wait."

His arms tightened around her, and he brought his lips close to hers. "No, I don't want to wait. This is right, and I want to get married as soon as we can arrange it."

"Okay."

They kissed, the warm pressure of his mouth making her heart sing.

Anton withdrew, but the tip of their noses almost touched. "I guess we need to start looking for rings."

"I guess so." Tamika bit her bottom lip, smiling hard.

Pulling her with him, Anton backed her toward the bathtub. "Ready for your shower? I'll help you."

"Oh, I need help now?"

"Yes, lots of help. That's what fiancés do. They help."

"You're gonna be late," she pointed out.

"I can be late one time," he said.

Minutes later, they were kissing and soaping each other in the shower. When they both left for work later, Tamika grinned all the way to the commercial kitchen.

She couldn't imagine life getting any better.

✿ 19 ✿

Tamika's phone rang, breaking her concentration. She lifted her gaze from the twenty-quart double boiler on the stove where she was stirring melting shea butter and beeswax with a spatula.

"Has anyone seen my phone?" she asked, glancing over her shoulder at the two workers.

After the initial spike in sales a couple of weeks ago, orders had settled into a steady stream, and she'd dropped down to two temps. Having them on board gave her more time to experiment with new product ideas, the part of work she enjoyed the most.

"Here you go," Kirk said. He worked at a stainless-steel table assembling makeup kits for the USPS pickup at the end of the day. The other temp was dropping cooled lip balm mixture into tubes with a pipette.

Kirk tossed her the phone, and she caught it.

"Thanks." Tamika didn't recognize the number, but since they were calling on her business cell, she assumed the call was about business. She answered quickly before the call went to voicemail.

"Hello, may I speak to Miss Tamika Jones, please," a woman's crisp voice said. "This is Inez Fernsby calling from the office of Sylvie Johnson of SJ Brands."

Shocked, Tamika stopped stirring. "I'm sorry, who is this?"

"Inez Fernsby. Is this Miss Jones? I'd like to talk to you about your cosmetics line," the woman said.

This had to be some kind of joke. Sylvie Johnson was a multi-billionaire who owned several businesses, including a cosmetics line specifically for women of color. Her products were sold in sleekly designed packages in high-end department stores around the world. Her name was synonymous with quality. Why the heck would she be calling TamCam Cosmetics?

Tamika rested a hand on her hip. "Okay, who are you really, and who put you up to this?"

The woman laughed. "My boss, Sylvie Johnson put me up to this. Your cosmetics line has come to her attention, and she asked me to extend an invitation to you, to visit her office and talk with her and her vice president of operations about a possible business arrangement."

Tamika pulled the phone away from her ear and stared at the screen. "No, seriously. Did Calvin put you up to this? Because it's not funny." Though she spoke with skepticism, her heart was beating faster and faster because the woman sounded professional and legit. Could this be real?

"Ma'am, I don't know who Calvin is," Inez said, speaking slowly, "but Ms. Johnson would like to see you on Friday, if you're free. If you're not and there's a better time, I have her schedule in front of me and can make the arrangements with you."

"You're serious?" Tamika squeaked.

Kirk, who was placing a tube of lipstick in one of the boxes, paused and frowned at her.

"Very. Ms. Johnson does not do this very often. She's a very busy woman. So if I were you, I'd make that appointment."

Tamika's knees weakened, and she gripped the counter beside the stove. After swallowing the ball of nerves in her throat, she asked, "What time on Friday?"

"This is a preliminary meeting, to talk to you about your product line. Therefore, it shouldn't last more than an hour, but more than likely will only last about thirty minutes. As I said, she's a very busy woman. I have an eleven o'clock and two o'clock opening. Which time works for you?"

Tamika's mind was racing. She could hardly think. "Um, eleven o'clock. No, no, change that to two o'clock," she added in a rush. She wanted as much time as possible to get ready for the visit.

"Good, I have you down for two o'clock on Friday. We'll send a car to pick you up. Where should I send the driver?"

Tamika gave the address.

"One moment, please." There was a slight pause before Inez resumed speaking. "Based on your location, I'll have the driver arrive at one-thirty, which will have you here in plenty of time for your meeting with Ms. Johnson. Her daughter, Ella Brooks, is the vice president of operations and will be in attendance, as well. Will anyone be joining you?"

"Um, no."

"I'll give you my direct number so that you can call me if you need to make any changes, including having your business partner or someone else in attendance." Inez rattled off her phone number. Tamika grabbed a lipstick from Kirk and scribbled the digits on the steel countertop.

"Do you have any questions for me?" Inez asked.

"No, no questions." Tamika was still in a state of shock and would probably have a million questions after she regained consciousness.

"Then I will see you on Friday at two o'clock. Enjoy the rest of your day, Miss Jones."

The line went dead, and Tamika stared at the blank screen. Sylvie Johnson wanted to talk to her about her cosmetics line and was sending a car to pick her up for the meeting. Was this real life?

"Is everything okay?" Kirk asked, frowning.

Tamika looked at him and her lips expanded into a wide grin. "Everything is better than okay."

◈

"WOULD YOU RELAX, YOU'RE DRIVING ME CRAZY!" ANTON said from the bed.

Tamika stopped pacing and glared at him. "I can't. I have a very important meeting tomorrow. Potentially life changing! When you received the call for an interview at Abraham, MacKenzie & Wong, were you relaxed?" Anton opened his mouth to answer, but she pointed a finger at him. "Don't answer. Knowing you, you were calm, cool, and collected and waltzed into the firm with confidence. I'm not going to compare myself to you." Hands on her hips, she resumed pacing.

"I was a little nervous, I admit, but I was confident because I was prepared. And you're prepared. Remember, they called *you*. If you ask me, they're the ones who are interviewing."

Tamika snorted. "Yeah, right. We both know that's baloney."

She stopped moving and looked down at the outfits she'd picked out and placed at the end of the mattress. She couldn't decide what to wear. She'd gone to the mall yesterday and bought a new dress—deep purple, with gold shoes and complementing accessories. As an alternative, she considered going the more conservative route, choosing a white ruffled blouse, and a black pencil skirt and jacket from her closet.

Anton left the bed and padded over, bare-chested, with the elastic waistband of his plaid pajama pants hanging low on his lean hips.

"You're stressing yourself out for no reason. Okay, maybe I exaggerated by saying you're interviewing them."

"*Maybe?*"

"But," he continued, ignoring her, "they called you for a reason, and that's because they saw potential in your products. Like I told you, Ms. Johnson is one of my firm's clients. She's a no-nonsense person. She wouldn't have called if she didn't see a way to make money with you. And I guarantee you she's already made up her mind and just needs to confirm that you're someone she wants to go into business with."

From what he'd said, the firm earned lots of money in billable hours handling Ms. Johnson's affairs. Anton didn't work with her directly because he was low down on the totem pole—too low to deal with such a high-profile, important client.

"In other words, this is for me to screw up," Tamika said.

"In other words, this is your opportunity to shine and confirm that she should be doing business with you."

Tamika placed her palms on his bare chest. "Is there any way you could let some of that confidence seep into me by osmosis?"

Anton chuckled and pulled her close. She nestled against his chest, melting into his strength and warm skin as her worries drained away.

"You got this, sweetheart," he whispered.

Tamika tipped back her head to look up at him. The differences between him and Calvin were stark. Her ex had been completely uninterested in her work, but Anton was not only helpful, he was her cheerleader.

"When I started my cosmetics business, I thought I'd always have to do it alone, and I never considered having someone partnering with me. Certainly not someone whose work I admire as much as this woman. If she takes me on, my business will explode."

"And that's what you want, right?"

Though fear corded in her stomach, Tamika nodded. "Yes, that's what I want. Going into business with Sylvie Johnson would be a dream come true."

"Then we're going to claim it, okay? No more doubts. And, you're going to come to bed and get a good night's rest. Tomorrow you'll put on your makeup and that purple dress, which I think is more your style than the conservative black and white suit. When the car comes to pick you up, you'll march into that office with your head held high, like you belong there."

"You know what, I might have to hire you for the job of hype man," Tamika said.

"How much does the position pay?" Anton asked.

"Unlimited sex and shoulder massages."

"I'll take it!" he exclaimed.

She laughed, and when he kissed her lips, she cradled his jaw in both her hands. "My luck has changed since I met you." She kissed his soft lips, sighing with happiness.

His hands reached around to cup her bottom. "Me too," he whispered against her mouth. "Life couldn't be better."

🕷 20 🕷

I n preparation for the meeting with Sylvie Johnson, Tamika misted her face with a blend she'd created made of rosewater, aloe, and glycerin. She was currently testing the new product and planned to add it to her website for the winter, marketing the spray as a way to hydrate the hair and skin, and as a pick-me-up during the day.

Refreshed, she dropped the two-ounce bottle into her purse and slipped on her shoes.

The driver arrived promptly at one thirty p.m. She expected a sedan or perhaps an SUV, but he arrived in a shiny black limo and held the door open for her as if she was a rock star. She slid onto the soft leather of the backseat and smiled to herself when she caught one of the neighbors staring at them.

Though tempted to drink the water or juice or try one of the snacks in the console, she opted not to indulge because of the queasy nervousness that hovered in her belly, and she didn't want to risk throwing up inside the limousine. Or worse, during the meeting.

The ride took twenty minutes, during which Anton sent a text wishing her good luck. She responded with multiple kissing face emojis.

After the driver dropped her off in front of the building, she was greeted by a young woman on the inside who inquired if she needed the restroom or any refreshments. Tamika declined both and was escorted to the top floor. As she was led into Ms. Johnson's suite of offices, she noticed the tomb-like quiet and responded by speaking in a hushed tone to her escort.

A woman rose to greet her. She was middle-aged, with blue eyes and shoulder length hair streaked with gray. Extending a hand, she said with a smile, "Hello, I'm Inez. We spoke on the phone."

"Hello, it's nice to meet you." Tamika shook her hand.

"Thank you, Leslie," Inez said to the young woman beside Tamika. Her escort nodded and left them alone. "I'll let Ms. Johnson know you're here. Please, have a seat."

Tamika sat on a contemporary-looking leather sofa and waited with her hands clasped on her lap while Inez spoke quietly into the phone. After she hung up, she came around her desk.

"She's ready for you. Right this way."

Tamika took a deep breath and followed her. Inez opened the door and let her enter one of the most well put together offices she had ever seen. There was plenty of white in the room, and she remembered once reading that white was Ms. Johnson's favorite color. Quite huge, the office contained an area where chairs that looked comfortable enough for a living room were grouped around a table filled with Tamika's products.

As Inez softly closed the door behind her, a woman, who looked like a younger version of Ms. Johnson—with the same narrow face, high cheekbones, and light-brown eyes that shone like gems against her dark skin—extended a hand to Tamika.

"Hello. I'm Ella Brooks, the vice president of operations."

"Tamika Jones," Tamika returned, breathing slowly and evenly as she shook her hand.

Despite being impressed by Ella, she was completely overwhelmed by the sight of the legendary Sylvie Johnson, who rose from her glass desk in front of the window and approached wearing a pair of black glasses.

She was shorter than her daughter, but with no less of a commanding presence. Regal in stature, with flawless dark brown skin and sharp, assessing topaz-colored eyes. She looked trim and fit in gold, wide-legged pants, a white high-collared shirt, and a gold brooch over her left breast. Tamika hoped she looked as good as Sylvie did when she was her age.

Sylvie removed her glasses. "Welcome. I trust you had no problems with the transportation we sent?"

"None at all." Tamika was proud of herself. Her voice wasn't shaking.

"Good. Please, join me and my daughter, Ella, over here. As you can see, we have some of your products on hand."

Actually, it looked like they'd purchased all of her products. Tamika sat down on the loveseat, and the two women sat on the sofa across from her. Lip balms, makeup kits, lipstick, eyeliner, and other products were spread out on the table.

"Thank you so much for agreeing to see us today, and on such short notice," Sylvie said.

Tamika almost laughed out loud. As if anyone would not drop everything to meet with her.

Sylvie continued. "We are very interested in your products and your creativity. But first, let me explain why you're here. Ella handles operations for my companies, including the cosmetics line. We have people who are constantly keeping an eye on the industry because we don't want to fall behind. We're a large company, but we pride ourselves on being nimble enough to change with the times.

"It so happened that the daughter of one of our marketing assistants—a freshman in college—found out about your Weekend Slumber Party kit and raved about it to her mother. The marketing assistant told her manager, which in turn caused TamCam Cosmetics to come up in a weekly meeting which my daughter oversaw. She looked into your products, read a recent article about you, and remembered a conversation we'd had before." She stopped speaking and turned to her daughter.

Ella took over. "My mother and I had discussed how to expand our market share." She picked up the Weekend Slumber Party kit, which contained eyeliner, mascara, two shades of lipstick, bronzer, and makeup remover pads in a rose gold pouch that closed with drawstrings. "We don't do things like this. It's very clever. Most of our products are in luxury stores, and they're considered a luxury, so they're high-end and out of the financial reach of many consumers. Most of our customers are in the thirty-five and older age bracket. What I discussed with my mother was expanding our market share by reaching out to a younger demographic—something you do very well. Teens learning to take care of their skin and experimenting with makeup. Young women in their early twenties and a little older, who are looking for more fun products, to whom more fun marketing and lower costs would appeal.

"We think your products, particularly your creativity when conceiving product lines, would be a way to tap into that demo-graphic. And, as these women eventually become older and earn a greater income, they will already be loyal customers who'll naturally gravitate toward the other product lines we have to offer."

"Essentially, we want to go into business with you and build on what you've started, to capture a younger demographic," Sylvie said. "Is that something you would be interested in?"

Oh my goodness, oh my goodness, oh my goodness! Tamika screamed internally.

"Yes ma'am, I would," she said calmly.

"That's what I wanted to hear. Now tell me, how do you handle your manufacturing?" Sylvie picked up a red-tinted lip balm. "For a product like this, for example?"

"Some items I outsource, like my eyeliner pencils, but my staff and I make the lip balm by hand, in a commercial kitchen," Tamika replied.

Sylvie nodded but frowned. "That could create inconsistent batches, but we'll work on that. We have the capacity to mass produce based on your formulations. The article and your website state your products are cruelty-free. Is that true?" She arched an eyebrow.

Tamika knew this was very important to Sylvie. Not only were her own products cruelty-free, she used only organic and all-natural ingredients. Customer raved that they often forgot they were wearing makeup and swore the products improved their skin.

"Yes. My suppliers are committed to that, and I only test the products on myself, friends, and other models."

"Good. In that case, I have no doubt we can do business together. We are very interested in partnering with you."

"When you say partnering, do you mean... like fifty-fifty?" Tamika asked.

"You would be okay with that?" Sylvie asked.

"Yes, ma'am," Tamika said quickly. This was a dream come true! She could potentially make millions with the investment and marketing power from SJ Brands.

Eyes narrowing, Sylvie slowly placed the lip balm on the table, and Ella shifted on the seat.

Internally, Tamika panicked. She had clearly said something wrong. All she'd done was agree. Should she have said something else? Was she being too greedy?

"My dear," Sylvie began, "TamCam Cosmetics is your baby, and *you* should retain control. My initial offer was going to be fifty-one/forty-nine, with you keeping fifty-one percent. But before we get deep into the numbers, you should hire legal counsel to help you with the negotiations. There are going to be a lot of changes, with your input, of course. But you, my dear, will need to have someone on your team protecting your interests. Because I assure you, I will be protecting mine. Do you understand?"

Tamika swallowed and nodded. "Yes, I understand."

"We will be investing quite a lot of money into your company. I hope you are prepared for what is to come."

"I am," Tamika said.

"Do you have any questions for us?" Ella asked.

"Nothing right now. I guess I'll wait to see what your offer is," Tamika said.

"We'd like to get started right away," Ella told her.

Tamika straightened her shoulders and sat up straighter in the chair. "As soon as you send over your offer, I'll run it by my attorney."

A slight smile lifted the corners of Sylvie's lips. "Good." She stood. "Thank you for coming. Ella will show you out."

They shook hands. Sylvie's was a firm handshake, but not overly done, and she looked Tamika directly in the eyes. She slipped on her glasses and strode back to her desk.

Tamika followed Ella out of the office.

At the elevator, Ella said, "Expect to hear from us very soon."

"Thank you," Tamika said.

"We look forward to doing business with you. Have a good day, Miss Jones."

I will now! she wanted to scream. Instead, she nodded, saying politely, "You do the same."

She entered the elevator and rode it all the way to the bottom. On the twenty-minute ride to the apartment, she sat quietly in the back seat of the limo, heart thumping, overwhelmed by the meeting, awestruck when she thought about how her life was about to change.

The driver dropped her off at the apartment, and after she let herself inside, she closed the door, leaned back against it—and screamed.

❧ 21 ❧

The day had arrived to talk to her father, and in a few minutes he'd knock on the door.

Tamika's father was from St. Kitts in the Caribbean, and as old-fashioned and protective as they come. He believed in gender roles, though he'd been insistent that she and her sister get a good education so they could take care of themselves. Somehow he never saw an issue with those conflicting ideologies.

She hadn't been home in a while, and there were other issues they needed to discuss before she broached the topic of her pregnancy, so Anton went to pick up lunch, giving her time to talk to her father alone.

She paced the floor, and when her father knocked, she hurried over and opened the door.

"Hi, daddy!" She flung herself into his arms.

Linwood Jones was a tall, burly man with a bald head and salt and pepper beard. As always, he was dressed casually, this time in jeans and a plaid shirt. He pulled her into a snug hug and squeezed her tight. Growing up he hadn't been affectionate, but after her mother's passing, the hugs became more frequent, and he often told her that he loved her.

He stepped back and took a good look at her. "You look happy," he said.

His deep voice still carried his lilting Caribbean accent.

"That's because I am happy."

"Good, good."

He entered and immediately began inspecting the apartment, eyes scouring the photos on the wall that now included pictures of Tamika and Anton together.

"Well, where is your young man?" he asked, turning to face her.

"I wanted to talk to you alone first. Have a seat." Tamika motioned to the sofa.

Linwood's eyebrows lifted in surprise. "Sounds serious," he said, sitting down.

"Would you like something to drink?" Tamika asked, purposely not responding to his comment.

"No, I'm fine."

She joined him on the sofa and folded her hands in her lap. Despite being a grown woman of twenty-nine years, her father's approval was very important to her.

"What do you think about the apartment?"

"It's nice, what I've seen so far. I'm glad you got rid of that Calvin fella."

"Yeah, me too," Tamika muttered.

"I warned you about playing house with that boy, didn't I? Didn't I warn you?" her father said, lifting a bushy eyebrow.

They were off to a bad start. "Yes, you did," Tamika answered dully.

Her father grunted. "Now you're doing the same thing with this other one—what's his name?"

"Anton," Tamika supplied, though she'd told him his name at least a dozen times before. She suspected her father was pretending not to know his name.

"Yes, Anton." Linwood shook his head.

"This situation is different."

"How is it different? I'm worried that this is a rebound thing, and not only for you but for him, too. You found comfort with each other after being cheated on. Nothing is wrong with that, but you didn't have to move in with him."

"I know, but at the time I didn't have anything."

"What you mean you didn't have anything?"

She winced at the affront in his voice. She hadn't told her father about Calvin stealing her money because she didn't want to hear another round of "I told you so." But since her life had turned around, unburdening her soul became easier. She told her father about her stolen savings and included the eviction. When she was finished, Linwood's eyebrows were pushed so far down over his eyes, he looked like a caricature of anger.

"Why didn't you tell me? You went through all of that and didn't say a word to me? We talk every week, Tam Tam."

"I know."

"Did you think I wouldn't help you?"

"I know you would have. That's the problem. You kept telling me to come home."

"And what's so wrong with that? You wouldn't have to worry about rent or bills. You know that. You could stay with me and find a job, save your money, and then go out on your own again."

"But that's not what I wanted."

Linwood sighed heavily and turned away from her. "I don't understand you," he muttered. "I would do anything for you, but you don't seem to want my help."

Tamika touched his forearm and brought his attention back to her. "I need to be able to do things on my own. To grow up. I need to be able to make mistakes and learn from them."

Growing up, her father had been so protective, she had practically lived in a bubble. She lived at home when she attended Augusta University, so moving to Atlanta had been the first time in her life that she'd been on her own, and she let loose in a way that she couldn't have while under his roof.

"And what exactly did you learn from that loser, eh? By the way, he better hope he never runs into me, I know that."

"I learned what it's like to be in a relationship that doesn't meet my needs. Yes, Anton and I are living together like Calvin and I did, but Anton is so much different. He's really good to me, daddy. He reminds me of you."

That caught his attention. He'd been frowning down at the floor but lifted his gaze to look at her. "You trying to sweet-talk me?" he asked.

"No," Tamika answered with a smile. "He really does remind me of you."

"How?"

"He's a protector and a provider. He's a really good man, and I'm lucky to have found him. I'm glad I know the difference between a good man and a bad one now."

Linwood sighed and leaned back against the sofa. "I want you to be happy, Tam Tam. You've been through a lot," he said in a grave voice.

"You, too," she said quietly.

"Yeah." Linwood nodded.

They both fell silent, quietly commiserating on their shared pain. She had lost her sister and mother. He had lost his daughter and wife.

"I'm not coming back home, daddy," Tamika said quietly.

He swallowed, and when he spoke, his voice was thick with emotion. "I know."

"And I'll be fine." She took his hand and gently squeezed. "You need to start dating."

Her father was protective, but part of his need to have her close was because he was lonely. She realized that and believed nudging him toward dating would help alleviate the loneliness he experienced in the house by himself.

"There's nothing out there for an old man like me," he grumbled.

"That's not true. People find love at any age, and you can,

too." She rubbed the back of her hand over his beard. "We need to clean up your beard a little and do something with these nails."

"I'm a *mechanic*."

"That's no excuse. You can still take care of your hands."

He harrumphed. "Well, tell me what to do, and I'll do it. You know all about that stuff."

"Deal." Tamika smiled, happy to have another project to work on. Her father would be okay. "Before you leave, I'll write down some instructions for you. Now, I have some good news. The negotiations are complete, and next week I sign the paperwork. I'll officially be in business with SJ Brands Cosmetics!"

"Whaaat! You did it? You know, I told Cindy in the office about your business deal. I hope you don't mind. She says that's the makeup she wears. It's expensive as hell, but she said it's the best makeup on the market. I have to tell her the good news. Tam Tam, I'm so proud of you." Linwood pulled her into a hug.

When he released her, she said, "And I have some more news."

"Oh my goodness. You giving me a heart attack today."

Tamika giggled and got up from the sofa. "Let me get you something to drink. I have to wait for Anton to get here. He should be back any minute with lunch."

She and her father talked for about ten minutes before she heard the key turning in the door. Tamika and her father stood up as Anton entered the apartment.

He walked over to them and set the food on the table.

"Hello, Mr. Jones. Nice to meet you." He extended his hand.

"Nice to meet you, too," Linwood said, inspecting him from head to toe.

Nervously licking her lips, Tamika edged closer to Anton. "The reason I wanted to wait until Anton came home is because what I have to tell you involves him, too. Daddy, you're going to be a grandfather. Anton and I are going to have a baby."

The smile on her father's face faltered and eventually died. "A baby?"

"I want this baby," Tamika quickly added.

Anton took her hand in his.

"Oh my goodness, why is everything so rushy-rushy? You can take your time. You two haven't been together that long."

"I love your daughter, Mr. Jones. I know everything I need to know about her."

Tears of appreciation sprang into Tamika's eyes, and she threaded her fingers through Anton's.

"He makes me happy. I'm *happy*. And he's going to be a great father, and a great husband."

"Husband?" Her father's eyes widened.

"Tamika and I are getting married." Anton briefly looked at her, love shining in his eyes. "We'd love to have your blessing."

Linwood ran his hands over his face. "That's a hard one."

"It doesn't have to be. Tamika told me that you had decided to marry her mother after your first date. The only reason you didn't ask for her hand is because you didn't want to scare her off. A good friend of mine told me that you'll know when you find the right woman, because no one else will do. Tamika is the right woman for me. I love her, and I'm happier than I've ever been. "

Hearing him profess his love to her father was almost her undoing. She didn't know how she kept the tears at bay.

"You did tell me he's a lawyer," Linwood said to Tamika. "He makes a good argument." He laughed softly in defeat.

"Do we have your blessing?" Tamika asked.

Her father's eyes softened. "You're the best of me, you know that? You ask me to do anything, and I'll do it. I know sometimes I can be overbearing, but it's only because I love you."

"I know."

Linwood stared at her with a wistful expression on his face. "So often I still think of you as my little Tam Tam, putting on your mother's lipstick and making a mess of her makeup. But you're not that little girl anymore, are you? You're Tamika—a grown woman with her own business, and now you're about to get married and become a mother. Where does the time go?"

He opened his arms, and she moved into them, and they held each other close.

"You have my blessing."

"Thank you, daddy."

"You take care of my little girl... I mean, grown woman daughter," Linwood said. He cleared his throat, eyes looking a bit misty.

"I'll do my best," Anton promised. "But the way her business is growing, she'll be the one taking care of me."

The three of them had a good laugh.

Then, over the course of lunch, Tamika watched the two men in her life talk and connect.

❦ 22 ❦

Tamika stood and shook hands with her attorney, as well as the attorneys for SJ Brands. Since the final negotiations had been handled days before, neither Sylvie nor her daughter were in attendance at the signing.

Sylvie hadn't gone easy on her, but in the end Tamika was satisfied with the terms. They agreed to a 57-43 ownership deal, and Tamika would have an office at the company's headquarters downtown, a small staff, as well as access to the offsite lab to work on new products.

She was excited and grateful, knowing that the deal could have been worse. She now understood how smaller companies could get taken advantage of by unethical business people. It would have been so easy for Sylvie to use her excitement from the first meeting against Tamika to ensure a more lucrative deal for herself. Instead, she'd given her advice, which in turn made Tamika want to do business with her even more.

Tamika wished her sister and mother could have been alive to see this day and how far she'd come, but she liked to think they knew what she'd accomplished and were proud of her.

She exited the office building, pulling out her phone as she marched with a spring in her step down the sidewalk. At a place around the corner, she was going to treat herself to a bowl of ice cream covered with strawberry and fudge syrup. But first she had to update Anton.

"How did everything go?" he asked upon answering the phone.

It was so good to hear his voice and share this special moment with him.

"You're talking to the new business partner of SJ Brands Cosmetics, baby!" Tamika squealed.

A woman coming in the opposite direction stared and arched her eyebrows.

"Woohoo! That's my girl," Anton said.

Grinning hard, Tamika couldn't be happier at his response. His support had been invaluable, and he was not in the least bit threatened by her pending success. On the contrary, he was constantly encouraging and supportive.

An unexpected pain whipped across Tamika's abdomen, causing her to draw a sharp breath and come to a sudden stop in the middle of the sidewalk. The man behind her bumped into her back.

"Sorry," he mumbled as he walked around her.

"What's wrong?" Anton asked.

Moving more slowly, Tamika massaged the underside of her belly where the pain had come from.

"I don't know. I had a sharp pain in my stomach from out of nowhere."

"You okay?" He was immediately on the alert.

Not wanting to worry him, she replied, "No, I'm fine. The pain is gone, actually. I don't know what could have caused it."

"Are you sure?"

"Yes, absolutely. I'm on my way to get myself some ice cream." Breathing easier, she picked up the pace to her destination.

"I'm going to knock off early tonight so I can take you to a nice dinner. We need to celebrate."

"Ooh, I like that idea. Can I pick the place or are you going to surprise me?"

"You can pick the place. Where do you want to eat?"

"I've always wanted to eat at the Sun Dial. Can we do that?"

The Sun Dial was an upscale restaurant on top of The Westin Peachtree Plaza. It slowly turned, giving a 360-degree view of the Atlanta skyline.

"As long as I've lived here, I've never eaten there either. Dinner at the Sun Dial will be something we can experience together for the first time."

Tamika stopped in front of the ice cream shop. "I like experiencing new things with you," she whispered.

"Me, too," Anton said, and by the sound of his voice she could tell he was smiling.

"I'll see you later. Go back to work. I called to let you know how the document signing went because I knew you'd be wondering. I'm calling my father next."

"Thanks. See you later."

"Love you." Tamika blew him a kiss.

"Love you, too."

Tamika moved to open the door of the shop, but her steps were cut short by another severe cramp in her abdomen. This time the pain was harsher and sliced into her lower back at the same time it cut across her belly. She let out a small cry and fell against the store's window, tears springing to her eyes as the pain cut a relentless path under her skin.

"Ma'am, are you okay?" a dark-haired young woman asked. Her brow furrowed as she and the man with her came closer.

"I-I'm not sure," Tamika gasped.

Then the shock of moisture in her underwear. Something wet and sticky, which filled her with dread.

The baby.

"Can I help you sit down somewhere?" the young woman asked.

Though she heard the question, Tamika was hardly paying

attention. It took all her energy to deal with the unusual sensation between her thighs and the pain consuming her midsection.

She hit redial on the phone with her thumb and shakily brought the device to her ear. Anton didn't answer. The phone rang and rang until his voicemail picked up.

Where was he? She'd talked to him only a minute ago.

"Anton," she gasped, tears filling her eyes. The young woman remained close by, face filled with concern. "Call me back, please. Something's wrong. I'm gonna have to go to the hospital. I-I think it's the baby."

❧

MARVIN AND ANTON STROLLED OFF THE ELEVATOR AFTER lunch. Craving Caribbean food thanks to Tamika, Anton had suggested they eat at a nearby Jamaican spot, but he didn't think the meal was up to par. Marvin had played safe and ordered wings and rice. Anton had ordered curry chicken and rice.

"She's got you spoiled, man," Marvin said, shaking his head.

Anton laughed softly. He couldn't deny the truth. "I can't lie, she's got me eating all kinds of stuff that I never thought I'd eat, and loving every bite. Her curry chicken is so good."

"Is it spicy, though?"

"Not at all. Full of flavor, you know what I mean? With spices and thyme and all kinds of good shit." He entered his office.

Marvin hovered in the doorway. "You eat curry goat, too?"

"Yep. She eased me into it—started with curry chicken first and then cooked goat one day. It's delicious, I'm telling you. She even got me eating cow foot now."

"*Cow's feet?* No way." Marvin wrinkled his nose.

Anton laughed. "It's not my favorite, but I like that, too." He shrugged.

"Okay, this is going to sound weird, but is she doing something to your skin, cause your skin has been looking great lately."

Anton touched his face, loving that his skin had noticeably improved.

"That's Tamika, too. My skin is moisturized and soft now."

"Let me see."

Marvin reached for his face, but Anton jerked away.

"I'm not letting you touch my face, man. My skin is soft. Trust me."

"I wanted proof, that's all. Erica is always getting on to me about taking better care of my skin. Why are women like that?"

"They want us to do better," Anton answered with a shrug. "Tamika mixes up her little concoction in the kitchen and puts it in a jar. I scoop out whatever I need and then slather it on."

"How long do you leave it on?" Marvin asked. He was frowning as he studied Anton's face, arms crossed over his chest.

"Fifteen minutes, once a week."

"Ask her to hook me up, would you?"

"I'll think about."

"Don't be greedy, man. I'll pay."

"I'll run it by her and see."

"Yeah, you do that," Marvin muttered, as Anton laughed.

His friend left and Anton walked around his desk and sat down. The voicemail light was flashing, so he checked his messages. The first one was a return call from an attorney at another firm. The second message was from Tamika, and his blood ran cold.

Anton jumped up from his chair and darted out of the office. He dialed Tamika's number and gripped the cell phone to his ear.

"Hey, you okay?" Marvin paused on his way to the copy room.

"It's Tamika. She left me a message. There's something wrong... I-I gotta go." Anton jumped into the elevator and punched the button for the first floor.

The drive to hospital seemed to take forever, and he almost didn't make it because he nearly sideswiped another car on the way. Finally, he was able to park and rushed into the hospital, his heart beating fast in his throat.

Tamika's message had scared the crap out of him. He couldn't stand the thought of her being alone and in pain. And their baby...

He ran up to the nurse's station. "Hello, I'm looking for Tamika Jones. She's here but I'm not sure what room she's in."

"Your name?" The nurse behind the desk said.

She was annoyingly calm, while he was yelling inside.

"Anton Bivens. I'm her fiancé."

The nurse typed on the keyboard in front of her, and then she looked up at him with eyes filled with sympathy. *Shit.* That look made his heart plummet to his feet.

"Room seven-oh-two. She's waiting for you."

Anton hurried down the hall and found Tamika's room. Looking through the glass window in the door, he saw her lying on the bed with her eyes closed. He took a deep breath to calm down. He needed to be strong for her.

He eased the door open, and she must have heard him because her eyelids creaked up.

"Hey," he whispered, sitting beside her. He took her hand in his.

"Hi." Her lower lip trembled. "We lost the baby."

So many emotions—disappointment, pain, rage. They all lanced through him at once.

Anton squeezed her hand. He didn't know what to say. What questions should he ask? He sat there, useless and helpless.

Tamika stared up at the ceiling. "Can't have it all, right?"

"Don't say that, sweetheart." Anton kissed the back of her hand.

She laughed a little, and a tear streaked out of the corner of her eye. Anton brushed it away with his finger.

"You need anything?"

She shook her head. "No."

To think, only a couple of hours earlier, they'd planned to

have dinner and celebrate her accomplishment. Now they were both suffering.

Why was the world so unjust? Hadn't they both suffered enough loss? She'd lost her mother and sister, he'd lost his brother, and now they'd lost their baby.

Except for those painful periods in their lives, they were nothing alike. Their personalities were different. He was more reserved, she was outgoing. He was cautious and preferred to think first. She preferred to act first and then deal with the fallout.

Despite their differences, he believed that sometimes people found each other because their lived experiences made them compatible—whether as friends or more intimately as lovers—even if on the surface they don't appear to be compatible.

Because of that, he knew they would get through this. As long as they were together, they'd get past this painful period and thrive. They had each other.

"I'm here, sweetheart. However you need me, okay?" Anton said, his voice thick with grief.

Tamika gave him a wan smile. "Thank you."

❦ 23 ❦

Anton entered the apartment after a one-hour workout at the complex's gym. He heard Tamika somewhere in the back and paused, bracing for the sight of her and the maelstrom of emotions that constantly existed inside his chest.

For the past eleven days he'd been walking around on eggshells, not knowing what to do with himself or what to say to make her feel better. One time, he caught her staring at a pair of toddler sandals she'd purchased a while back. She didn't hear him enter the room and sat there cradling the shoes against her belly like they were a baby. Watching her had gutted him, and he regretted all the times he'd teased her about spending too much money on baby items.

At some point all the baby clothes, shoes, and toys disappeared from the apartment, as if they'd never been there in the first place. He didn't have the guts to ask Tamika what she'd done with them. Has she thrown them out or stored them in another location?

Since she left the hospital, every time he'd tried to get her to talk, she shut him down, and the last thing he wanted to do was add to the sadness in her eyes. She used to talk all the time, but since the miscarriage, she didn't talk much at all.

At least her work wasn't suffering. During her transition period with SJ Brands, she'd suspended purchasing on her website, and a landing page announced changes to come, encouraging visitors to join her mailing list. Most of her work consisted of conversations on the phone, doing interviews and planning. She'd gone into her new office once for a face-to-face meeting and for the most part acted normal, but he knew she wasn't well. The problem was, he couldn't get her to talk to him, and he didn't want to push too hard.

He went to work each day, going through the motions of taking care of his clients. He was doing such a good job, no one noticed a difference. Only Marvin knew that they'd lost the baby, and that was because he'd seen Anton rush out of the office. He told Anton about a miscarriage he and Erica had also suffered and spouted statistics about how often they happened, none of which helped. What helped was staying numb and pretending everything was okay.

Anton entered the bedroom and found Tamika sitting on the end of the bed, staring off into space. She wore the red cap she'd worn when she showed up at his apartment with the baseball bat, looking for her ex.

As he entered, she immediately perked up and smiled. She was pretending, too.

"Had a good work out?" she asked.

"Yeah."

They stared at each other in silence. Unspoken words and unexpressed grief hanging between them.

"What's wrong?" Tamika asked.

This was his opening, an opportunity to get her to talk. "Is there anything I can do?" he asked.

Her face fell. "I'm fine."

"You keep saying that you're fine, but I don't know if I should believe you."

"Do you want me to lie to you?" Tamika rubbed her hands up and down her thighs and then jerked to her feet. "Actually, we need to talk. I, um... I called Layla. I'm going to stay at her place for a while."

The words landed like a blow to his solar plexus, robbing him of air. "What? You're leaving? We should talk about this, Tamika."

"There's nothing to talk about. The baby is gone, and I need... a break, okay?" Her eyes were pleading with him.

Anton swallowed down the hurt of rejection. This wasn't about him. This was about her. He had to remember that. "How long will you be gone?"

She shrugged. "I don't know... a couple of days, that's all. I need my friends right now."

Damn. Another blow. More rejection.

He nodded. "Okay," he replied, trying to be understanding but not really understanding. They should be in this moment together, sharing their pain and talking to each other, but she was shutting him out.

"Do you need me to take you?" He couldn't help himself. Despite her making it obvious she didn't need him, the desire to take care of her remained strong.

Tamika shook her head. "No, I'm fine. I can drive. I'm leaving in a few minutes."

"Today?" Anton asked, shocked.

"Yes." She averted her eyes. "I packed a suitcase while you were gone."

Anton turned away from her. Obviously, she didn't need him. "Okay. Call me when you get there."

"I will."

From the corner of his eye, he saw her walk into the closet. She came out with a large suitcase and overnight bag. Did she need all of that for only a couple of days? He wanted to help her carry the bags but suspected she wouldn't accept his help.

Tamika paused, turning at the door. "I'll call you... once I get my head right."

"Yeah."

His body tensed as he fought the urge to run over and lift her into his arms. To hold her tight and kiss away the sorrow in the depths of her eyes.

After she left, the apartment became extra quiet. Being there alone was so much different than it used to be. He used to welcome time alone. Now, he avoided it because he craved the interaction with Tamika. She brightened his day. She made him laugh.

Anton trudged over to the nightstand on his side of the bed and reached in the back. He removed a black velvet box and lifted the lid. They'd never gone ring shopping together, but he'd gone alone. The day she miscarried, he'd planned to ask her to marry him at the Sun Dial, since he'd secretly purchased this ring a few days before. He'd told the jeweler he wanted a ring that was big, bold, and sparkled like her personality. She'd recommended this oval halo diamond ring with a pave setting. It was perfect for Tamika.

He set down the box, dropped onto the mattress, and buried his face in his hands. He didn't want to be here at home, alone, thinking about everything they had lost, barely able to breathe, as if his chest had caved in on him.

He may not understand the emptiness inside Tamika, but there was an emptiness inside of him, too. He'd been looking forward to their baby. His parents had been excited. He'd thought about buying a house, a major decision he hadn't considered before all of this happened. He was ready to get married and build a family with her and had already inquired at work about taking leave when the baby was born so he could spend time with him or her and Tamika. He was actually ready to be a dad, and no one was more surprised than he was.

When his brother died, he'd stifled the pain, pushing it down for years. He'd hardly talked about his brother's death with anyone for years. Thanks to Tamika, he learned that wasn't the best decision and opened up, talking more often about Ricky and their childhood, sharing the good times and sad times and times in between.

Now that he'd suffered another loss, he wanted to talk. He needed to. He needed Tamika.

But she wasn't here for him to talk to.

⚜

"Hey, I'm back," Layla called from the front, "and I brought Elijah with me."

"I'm in the kitchen," Tamika called out.

Both Elijah and Layla came to the open kitchen.

"Hi, Elijah."

"Hi, Tamika."

Elijah had dark skin and wore his loosely curled hair in a low fade. At first, Tamika thought he was too slick and reminded her of Layla's ex, Rashad—a smooth-talking playboy who broke her heart. But Layla's relationship with Elijah continued to blossom, and she generally seemed content, so Tamika dismissed her own reservations and concentrated on being happy for her friend.

"I stopped in to get some clothes," Layla explained.

"You guys hungry? I made breakfast for dinner. Pancakes, sausage, and eggs." Tamika used the spatula to point at the sausage and pancakes on the counter. She was in the process of scrambling eggs to go with the meal.

"Were you planning to feed an army?" Elijah asked, gaze on the plates of food.

Tamika laughed. "No, smarty pants. But I figured I'd make enough to have breakfast for a couple of days, too."

If she were still at the apartment with Anton, he'd help her eat all this food. She'd be lucky to have any left for breakfast in the morning.

"We're going out to eat. Want to join us?" Layla asked.

Tamika shook her head and wrinkled her nose. "And be a third wheel? No, thanks."

"You won't be a third wheel, and you're welcome to come, if you like. My treat," Elijah said. Then he disappeared from the doorway, leaving Layla and Tamika alone.

"He's a good guy," Tamika remarked. She'd had her doubts before, but maybe he wasn't so bad.

"Mhmm." Layla came over and leaned her hip against the counter. "Have you talked to *your* good guy today?"

"No, I haven't. But I will." She stirred the eggs.

"You need to call him, Tamika."

"I will, I promise. Not right now, though."

Layla fell silent. Then she leaned in. "You want to go out? I can ditch Elijah and we can go do something."

"You don't have to do that."

"I don't like you being here alone. Let's go to dinner or something."

Tamika forced a laugh and gestured to the food on the counter. "This is my dinner." She quickly looked away from the concern in Layla's eyes.

"How are you holding up?"

"Stop." Tamika set down the spatula and took a deep breath. The anger and frustration simmering near the surface bubbled up in a flash of heat. "I want everyone to stop asking 'How are you holding up?' 'How are you doing?' 'Are you okay?' You, Dana, my dad, Anton, my aunt, my cousins. It's exhausting! How many times do I have to say that I'm fine?"

Every time someone asked those questions, she wanted to scream because she didn't want to think about losing the baby. If she didn't think about the baby, then she could function semi-normally.

Layla fell silent and folded her arms across her midsection. Her neutral expression didn't convey whether or not she was upset.

Tamika's cheeks burned with shame at her outburst. "I'm sorry. I didn't mean to yell."

"You went off a little bit, but you didn't yell. I won't ask you that question anymore. If you say you're fine, then I accept what you say. But if anything changes and you want to talk, you know I'm available."

Tamika swallowed down the pain. Despite her protestations that she was fine, she was still sorting through her feelings and didn't know how to express them to anyone. "I know."

Layla rested a hand on her shoulder. "I'm going to get my clothes and then Elijah and I are leaving."

"Thanks for letting me stay here. I appreciate it."

"Of course. You're one of my best friends."

Layla pulled her into a brief hug and left the kitchen. Tamika took a plate of eggs, pancakes, and sausage out to the dining table with orange juice.

Soon afterward, Layla came out of the bedroom with her bag. "We're leaving now," she announced.

"You guys have fun. See you in a couple of days." Tamika forced a smile. She'd gotten good at that lately—forcing smiles. Pretending to be happy.

"Maybe," Elijah said with a wicked grin, taking Layla's bag and then flinging an arm around her shoulders.

After they left, Tamika couldn't stand the quiet and turned on the television.

She would be fine, wouldn't she? She just needed time.

She stared at the plate. She stared at her phone beside the plate. There were several missed calls from Anton—calls she hadn't returned. She didn't know what to say to him. Sometimes she was okay, especially when busy with work. But during moments like this, she swore she was about to crack wide open.

Tamika sliced into the stack of pancakes and placed a forkful into her mouth. She chewed without enthusiasm. The normally delicious food tasted like rubbery sandpaper. She forced the pancake down her throat and followed with a swallow of orange juice.

Unable to eat another morsel, she left the meal on the table and went to lie down on the sofa, pulling a throw over her body. Curling into a ball, she closed her eyes.

She missed Anton and wasn't fine or good or any of the other lies she'd told. Today she saw a pregnant woman walking into a drugstore and seconds later burst into uncontrollable tears. She had to pull over on the side of the road and must have cried for thirty minutes before she was able to pull herself together and continue the drive to Layla's.

She longed to feel better, more like herself. To do that, maybe she needed to let loose and expel all the sorrow and rage and jealousy that threatened to suffocate her.

❧ 24 ❧

Anton slowly sipped his Black Russian in the VIP section of a popular club, celebrating the birthday of one of his co-workers with friends and staff from Abraham, MacKenzie & Wong.

The thumping music and flashing lights caused a minor headache, but what else did he have to do but toss back drinks and eat overpriced appetizers? Going home to an empty apartment was not at all appealing. And maybe, just maybe, he could self-medicate with alcohol to ease the pain of losing their baby and pining for Tamika.

He'd found the missing baby items stuffed in the back of the closet in the spare bedroom. Bags and bags of clothes and toys, cute little bows and headbands. He could almost hear Tamika now, *"Just in case we have a girl."*

He'd sat in the closet and stared at the bags for a long time before he realized that tears had leaked onto his cheeks. Finally, he stuffed them back in the corner, out of sight—his chest aching, his head pounding.

What was Tamika doing now? She was his heart. Without her, there was nothing there. His chest was... empty.

He stuffed a mini pizza-looking appetizer in his mouth and

practically swallowed it without chewing before grabbing another one and shoving it in his mouth, too.

"Damn, bruh, slow down," a male paralegal said beside him.

"Leave him alone," admonished an attorney in family law. She flashed him an extra friendly smile, the third for the night, but he had zero interest.

He was about to say something smart to the paralegal, when the guy nudged his shoulder. "Yo, ain't that your girl?"

Anton had placed a photo of Tamika on his desk, but he seriously doubted the paralegal was correct. Yet when he turned his head, he went ramrod straight in the chair, staring in disbelief. Tamika was on top of the bar shaking her ass with a martini glass in hand.

Stunning as usual, her pixie cut and makeup were immaculate. The sparkly short-shorts showed off her shapely legs in a pair of strappy black heels, and the gold sleeveless top clung to her torso and bared her toned arms. She was surrounded by men who gazed up at her with wolfish grins and cheers of encouragement.

"Yeah, that's her," Anton said grimly, getting to his feet.

He hadn't seen Tamika since she left their apartment to stay with Layla—bringing his life to a standstill—as if the Earth had literally stopped rotating on its axis.

She'd promised to call when she got her head right. She called once and then he never heard from her again. When he called, she didn't answer the phone or respond to his voicemails.

He'd parked in front of Layla's building twice in the past couple of days, having every intention of going up to the apartment and forcing Tamika to come home with him. But each time he'd driven away, chiding himself that he needed to give her time. Let her breathe and work through her loss.

"What are you about to do?" his friend asked.

"Get her down from there."

Anton marched over to the group and, using his elbows and height, shouldered his way between the ogling men until he stood directly in front of Tamika. When she saw him, her smile quavered like a kid caught in the act of disobeying their parent.

"Get down," he yelled, to be heard above the music, extending a hand to her.

She shot him a look of defiance and screamed, "I'm having fun!" Then she took a big gulp of her drink, tossing her head back to drain the contents.

The men roared their encouragement.

Anton moved closer, but a thicker, shorter man with red hair shoved him back. "Hey man, back up. She's having fun, we're having fun. Go be a buzzkill somewhere else."

"Yeah," another man beside him said, glaring at Anton.

"Get out of my way," Anton growled, wanting very badly to tear something up, and if it happened to be the faces of these two jerks, then so be it.

The short one stepped closer. "Make me." His breath reeked of beer, and Anton turned up his nose in disgust.

"Get the fu—" He pushed the redhead, and they ended up in a shoving match.

"Hey!" Tamika yelled.

Gingerly, she stepped off the bar onto one of the stools. With the help of another man, she hopped to the floor and placed herself between both Anton and the redhead.

"Chill!" she said to the stranger.

Anton placed an arm around her waist and whispered, "You're coming with me."

Without waiting for a response, he took her arm and shoved his way through the crowd. At first, he wasn't sure where he was headed, but then he saw the glowing restroom sign and crossed the dance floor in that direction.

He pulled Tamika into the men's bathroom, and she shoved his chest, dark eyes flashing.

"What the hell, Anton!"

"What the hell? I should be saying that to you. What do you think you were doing?"

The toilet flushed and a Black guy exited with a scowl on his face. "This is the men's bathroom. Y'all take that outside."

"Why don't you go outside and let me talk to my girl?"

"I don't want to talk to you." Tamika crossed her arms.

The other man laughed at him and took his time washing his hands while Anton silently fumed. When he finally left, he checked the stalls and then locked the door.

"What's going on with you? I've called you no less than ten times in the past week and you haven't returned a single call."

"I've been busy."

"Doing what? Dancing on top of bars again?"

"Leave me alone, Anton."

"How am I supposed to do that?"

He hadn't been able to leave her alone since they met. Lucky for him, she'd said yes to them moving in together.

"Easy. Stop calling." Arms still crossed, Tamika paced away from him. At least she didn't try to leave.

"Talk to me, Tamika."

In the reflection of one of the mirrors, he saw her bottom lip tremble.

Anton eased closer but kept his distance, when all he wanted to do was gather her in his arms and ease her pain. In retrospect, it was clear how much the miscarriage had devastated her, even as she said, *I'm fine.*

They'd prayed for a little girl. She, because she imagined doing her daughter's hair and makeup, getting her ready for prom, and watching her grow into an intelligent young woman— all the rites of passage mothers and daughters share through life. The friendship and love she'd shared with her own mother was the template she wanted to follow. He'd wanted a little girl because he wanted whatever Tamika wanted.

Few people understood their relationship. They were like night and day. He was the stuffy corporate attorney, she was the dynamic chemist whose mail-order business was about to become a multimillion-dollar empire. She was also the love of his life, and moving in together had been the best decision he'd ever made.

Their time apart had been hard. He missed her—his best friend, his source of laughter, her smile and vivacious personality making every day a good day.

"Talk to me. We used to talk about everything," Anton said quietly.

Tamika looked at him, arms still folded protectively around her midsection. Her eyes became glassy with tears, and he could no longer resist the need to comfort her. He closed the space between them with two long strides and wrapped her in his arms. He whispered soothing words as she quietly sobbed into his shoulder.

Someone jiggled the doorknob, but he ignored them, running one hand up and down her back.

When she stopped crying, she looked up at him with red eyes and a trembling smile. "Why do you put up with me?"

"Guess I love you."

She laughed and swiped at the wetness on her cheeks. "I needed time away."

"From me?"

"From me. From the utopia I'd created in my head of you, me, and our baby. Late night feedings..."

"Changing dirty diapers..."

"Tired from lack of sleep..."

"Staying up all night and staring at her when we should be sleeping when she sleeps." He smiled through the punch of pain in his chest.

"I wanted all of it. The good, the bad, the dirty, the cranky, the pretty, the cuteness, the..." She choked and swallowed. "I never wanted anything so much."

Anton cupped her face in his hands. He knew better than to say they could try again. All he could do was let her know that he would be there to support her. They'd both been through heavy losses before, and they could get through this, too. Together.

"I love you, Tamika. You don't have to bear this alone."

She gazed at him with grateful eyes. "I know. I'm sorry."

He kissed her lids and pulled her into another firm hug. "Let's go home. Okay?"

Sniffling, she nodded against his chest.

Someone banged so hard on the door Anton was certain he'd heard the frame crack.

"Hey! Anybody in there?"

"Let's go before they call security," Anton said.

Tamika giggled and rubbed her eyes dry. Taking his hand, she swung open the door. Two men stood outside. One scowled and the other raised an eyebrow.

"Sorry, gentleman. He's so irresistible, I couldn't wait until we got home."

Anton smirked as he walked by the men and then flung an arm around Tamika's shoulder.

Life would finally get back to normal.

❧ 25 ❧

"You should be yelling at me."

Tamika sat on the bed while Anton crouched before her and carefully removed the shoe from her right foot.

"I'm not going to yell at you," he said.

"What did I do to deserve you?" she asked.

"Hell if I know," he replied, grinning up at her from his lowered position.

When both shoes were off, they stood and Tamika started unbuttoning his shirt.

"What are you doing?" he asked.

"Undressing my man," she said.

She tugged the tail of his shirt out of his slacks and shoved it off his shoulders. She removed his undershirt and dropped that to the floor, as well. Then she smoothed her hands up his chest, over his nipples and his pecs until they came together around the back of his neck. Heat flared in his eyes as she pressed up against him.

"I love you," she said.

"I love you, too." Anton's arms slipped around her waist.

Tamika looked deeply into his light-brown eyes. "I know

we've already talked, but there's something else I need to tell you. I should've stayed here and talked to you, and I'm sorry that I didn't."

"I understand."

Gosh, he was such a good guy. "I know you do, but that doesn't excuse what I did. You were hurting, too."

"Not like you."

"Yes, like me. But in a different way. I allowed my grief to take over, and I forgot that you were grieving, too. I promise that won't happen again."

Anton kissed her forehead.

"Are *you* okay?" Tamika asked softly.

A deep, bone-tired sigh escaped him, and she lowered her arms so that they wrapped around his trunk instead. Rubbing her palms up and down his bare back, she whispered, "Take as much time as you need."

Anton's arms tightened around her, and he pressed his face into the side of her neck.

They stood still and held onto each other for an eternity while she absorbed his pain, giving comfort and providing the solace that he needed.

Finally, Anton whispered, "I missed you."

Tears sprang to her eyes. "I missed you, too."

She'd missed him but couldn't face him or the mess she'd made with her absence. She'd needed him but was too ashamed to reach out, yet he was right there, ready to forgive and take her hand, offering support as always.

She kissed his jaw and his Adam's apple. She missed the smell of him and welcomed the firmness of his muscles under her palms.

Her fingers pressed into his skin, and she let out a little moan as her tongue licked out to taste the underside of his chin. His right hand cupped her breast through her top, and his thumb brushed across the peak with erotic negligence. In response, her nipples tightened and the cleft between her thighs pulsed with need.

Slowly, they edged toward the bed. Tamika undressed him, Anton undressed her, and their clothes whispered to the floor in the quiet. The only sound that could be heard was their breathing. Then they climbed into bed with their lips and hands moving carefully, lovingly over each other's skin.

Initially, Tamika's actions were gentle and slow. But the kisses soon deepened, and the touches became more feverish. She smoothed her palms down his chest to his pelvis, stroking his stiffened length before she kissed it and licked the veined underside, reveling in the sound of his groans of satisfaction.

His fingers threaded through her dark hair, and his lips traced a path from the beating pulse at the base of her neck down through the valley between her breasts. His large hands closed around the full orbs and squeezed, kneading them with gentle force, adding to the teasing with prolonged sucks and moist licks of his tongue.

Slowly but surely, her breathing became more erratic— shifting from slow and labored to impatient, moaning pants. When Anton finally pushed inside of her, Tamika released a wild sigh of relief and closed her eyes to completely immerse herself in the sensation of his deep penetration.

Anton's fingers gripped her buttocks as he withdrew and then sank into her.

"Love you so much, sweetheart," he rasped in her ear.

"Love you, too. I love you, Anton!"

Tamika cried out the words as she orgasmed, gripping his shoulder blades, her legs wrapped around his waist. Her fingers tightened into fists as her body convulsed with pleasure. There was nothing but bliss as she floated among the clouds, her love for Anton filling every crevice of her heart.

"It's too late to be doing this," Tamika said.

After making love, they'd taken a shower. They were both craving pizza, but all the restaurants were closed at that time of the night, so they went to the grocery store and picked up two frozen pepperoni pizzas, which they promptly tossed in the oven for a very late-night meal.

"It's never too late for pizza," Anton told her.

Instead of sitting at the table, they reclined on the floor, like they did that first night months ago. She had fallen in love with him then but hadn't realized it at the time.

"We never did go on that celebration dinner after I signed the contracts," Tamika said, shaking Parmesan cheese over her slice.

"You ready to do that?" Anton asked.

"Yes, I'm ready."

She was ready for a lot of things. She was also ready to talk about the miscarriage, which they spent the next few minutes doing, sharing their thoughts and heartbreak. There were tears, but not as many as before. When they finished talking about the baby, they changed the conversation and discussed her plans for TamCam Cosmetics, and her hopes and dreams for the line now that she had the backing of a large industry player behind her.

"I can't wait to see my products in stores," Tamika said.

"Me, either. I'm making sure everybody knows—that's friends, family, and co-workers—that my girl—"

"Fiancée," she corrected.

"Fiancée." His smile lit up her heart. "Make sure they know all about my fiancée's products, and if they know what's good for them, they'll buy them."

"You're going to threaten them, Anton?" Tamika said with a laugh.

"Not threaten, but definitely give them a hard nudge."

"Please don't alienate your friends or lose your job pushing my products," Tamika said with a giggle.

"Speaking of which, Marvin was praising my skin a while

back and asked for some of that homemade moisturizing mask you put on my face."

"You mean my goop?"

"Don't start. I haven't called it goop since that first day."

"True. I'll make up a batch for him and pass on the recipe so he can make it himself at home."

"You mean so Erica can make it for him?"

"However they make that work, yes. But you're right, there's no way Marvin is mixing product to make a mask." Tamika giggled, shaking her head.

She chewed on a pepperoni slice and then asked Anton about work. Without disclosing confidential information, he told her about a few new cases that he'd picked up.

When they'd almost finished eating, Anton announced, "I can't stand it anymore. I'll be right back."

Confused, Tamika watched as he went toward the bedroom. Her back was to him as he came back, and before she could turn around, he came down behind her, palm extended in front of her. Tamika let out a small cry and her hands flew to her mouth when she saw the box.

"Oh my goodness, is that what I think it is?"

"Yes." Anton kissed her ear. "Will you marry me, Tamika Jones?"

"We were supposed to go ring shopping together." She turned to face him.

"I couldn't wait."

She opened the box and inside was a brilliant halo diamond ring, with smaller diamonds in the shank. "Oh my god. Baby, I love it."

Anton slipped the ring on her finger and she gazed at it in open-mouthed appreciation.

Tamika flung her arms around Anton's neck and kissed him hard. He pulled her onto his lap so that she straddled him, opening his mouth and sliding in his tongue to deepen the kiss.

"It's perfect. It's so me."

"Do I know my woman or do I know my woman?" Anton said.

"You know your woman." Tamika wiggled on his lap, and he groaned, grabbing her ass.

As they sat there in the near darkness, with only the light in the kitchen on, talking and laughing and teasing each other, Tamika had a sense of déjà vu. They'd done this before—connected on a deeper level—in a different place, at a different time.

But this time, their connection was stronger.

ABOUT THE AUTHOR

Delaney Diamond is the USA Today Bestselling Author of sweet, sensual, passionate romance novels. Originally from the U.S. Virgin Islands, she now lives in Atlanta, Georgia. She reads romance novels, mysteries, thrillers, and a fair amount of nonfiction. When she's not busy reading or writing, she's in the kitchen trying out new recipes, dining at one of her favorite restaurants, or traveling to an interesting locale.

Enjoy free reads and the first chapter of all her novels on her website. Join her mailing list to get sneak peeks, notices of sale prices, and find out about new releases.

Join her mailing list
www.delaneydiamond.com

f facebook.com/DelaneyDiamond
twitter.com/DelaneyDiamond
BB bookbub.com/authors/delaney-diamond
pinterest.com/delaneydiamond